A Textbook of English for Engineers and Technologists

a skills approach

Course authors
Humanities and Social Sciences Division
Anna University, Chennai

Course consultants
English Department
Thames Valley University
(formerly, Ealing College of Higher Education)
London

This book has been published by
Orient BlackSwan
www.orientblackswan.com

This book is the outcome of an English Language Teaching Project undertaken by the Division of Humanities and Social Sciences, Anna University, Chennai, as part of a collaborative programme between the governments of India and the UK.

ORIENT LONGMAN PRIVATE LIMITED

Resitered Office
3-6-752 Himayatneger, Hyderabad 500 029 (A.P.), India

Other Offices
Bangalore / Bhopal / Bhubaneshwar / Chennai
Ernakulam / Guwahati / Hyderabad / Jaipur / Kolkata
Lucknow / Mumbai / New Delhi / Patna

First Published 1999
tenth impression 2003

ISBN 81 250 1724 0

Typeset by Images, Chennai 600 011

Printed at Orion Printers, Hyderabad 500 004

Published by Orient Longman Private Limited
3-6-752 Himayatnager, Hyderabad 500 029

Acknowledgements

The publishers are indebted tothe following for permission to use copyright material: *Computers Today:* The Directorate of Gobar Gas Scheme, Khadi and Village Industries Commission, Gandhinagar, Bombay; The government of India Tourist Office; *The Hindu,* including *Survey of Indian Industry* 1986; *Indian Express; New Today; New Industrial Products*: Research and Development, produced by Agarwal Consultancy Bureau; *Appropriate Technology*, volume 14:2; *The AT Reader* published by Oxford University Press, India; *Business India*; The Centre for Science and Environment; *Fortune India*; the extract from *Encounters with Animals* by Gerald durrell, published by Granada Publishing Ltd; India *Today; New International; Parade magazine; Soviet Land; Span magazine; Technocrat; The Week*.

The publishers are grateful to the following for the use of photographs on the pages cited:

The Unesco Courier (1, 120); *The Magazine* and Sudarshan Khanna (28); Tata Burroughs Ltd. (42) *Span Magazine* (00, 171); George Francis (89, 132, 140, 157, 195, 234); *American Review* (218).

Every attempt has been made to contact holders of copyright, and sources have been acknowledged at each point where teh texts appear in the book. The publisher would be glad to hear from copyright holders not listed here to enable them to make due acknowledgement in future editions of this book.

Foreword

This book is the outcome of a project undertaken by Anna University in collaboration with the Overseas Development Administration of the United Kingdom and the British Council.

The book has been designed for the use of undergraduate students of engineering and technology who use English in different settings and for different purposes. The aim of the course is to impart to the students the skills that they need in their academic, and later in their professional, pursuits.

It is generally admitted that the old course materials, comprising anthologies of prose selections, and the old methodology, based mainly on the classroom lecture, are not conducive to the development of study skills and communicative competence in the students. There is, therefore, a need to develop an appropriate course in English for students of engineering and technology and to adopt an innovative approach to English language teaching and learning. This is the rationale behind the present book.

The counterpart institution in the United Kingdom which collaborated in this project is Thames Valley University (formerly, Ealing College of Higher Education), London. Mr Rod Ellis helped in the formulation of the project, and Ms Pauline Barr, Ms Susan Axbey and Mr Richard Hornsey visited Anna University as consultants on the project, planning and monitoring the progress of the work. I would like to thank them for the earnestness and commitment which they have shown in assisting the faculty of the University. I must also record our gratitude to the Overseas Development Administration, the British Council, London, and the British Council Divison in South India, for their contribution, both in material and expertise, to the project. Mr Robert Bellarmine, English Studies Officer, British Council Division in South India, was instrumental in coordinating the work of the project teams at Ealing and Anna University. I must express my deep appreciation of his contribution. Mr Alan Maley and Mr Roger Budd of the British Council Division in South India extended their support to the project in liberal measure and I would like to thank them most sincerely.

The project coordinator in Anna University was Dr V R Narayanaswami. The materials were produced by a group led by Mr T K Subramaniam. I compliment the members of the staff of the Humanities and Social Sciences Division of Anna University on their excellent work in bringing out this book. I am confident that the use of this textbook accompanied by the adoption of a learner-centered approach in the classroom will develop in students of engineering and technology the relevant study skills and provide practice in the communicative use of English.

Anna University
Madras

V C KULANDAISWAMY
Vice-Chancellor

Preface

This book was prepared by the staff of the Division of Humanities and Social Sciences as part of a special English Language Teaching Project for use by students of degree courses in engineering and technology.

It marks a departure from the conventional textbook such as an anthology of prose selections. It also presupposes a shift in the philosophy of English language teaching which has been in practice till now. With the conventional textbook the English class was mostly teacher-centered. The method of teaching was mainly lecture-oriented. The new materials are task-based and skills-oriented. They demand an actual use of the English language by students in the classrooms and encourage interaction among them.

We acknowledge with gratitude the permission granted by the authors concerned to use their material in the preparation of the reading texts in this book. In this context, we would particularly like to thank *The Hindu* on whose published material we have drawn liberally.

We are grateful to the British Overseas Development Administration and the British Council Division, Chennai, for their generous financial and administrative support of the project. We particularly wish to thank the course consultants, the staff of the English Department, School of Language Studies, Thames Valley University (formerly, Ealing College of Higher Education), London, for their valuable guidance and help in the preparation of this book.

We are indebted to our Vice-Chancellor Dr V C Kulandaiswamy for his sustained encouragement and support at every stage of the project.

Staff of the Humanities and
Social Sciences Division
Anna University

Introduction to the materials

The course materials presented in this book are meant for use by students of degree courses in engineering and technology. They are organised around five topic areas, namely, Energy, Computers, Technology, Environment and Industry. The topics have been chosen taking into account the needs and interests of students. The exploitation of each of these topics is done in such a way that interest and motivation are maintained and a balanced programme of carefully graded activities is offered. Each topic comprises three units, each of which provides work for four contact sessions.

The teaching of mixed groups of students with a wide range of abilities in English always presents a considerable challenge to English departments in our universities and colleges. The design of these materials offers a way of answering this challenge by providing special guidance and support for weaker students. Each unit consists of a main section (Parts 1 and 2) to be tackled by all students. The support materials in the form of Preparation and Follow-up sections are designed to help slow learners cope with the main section.

The work in these materials is task-based and skills-oriented. A range of language functions of particular relevance to engineering and technology is exemplified in the texts for reading and listening, and practised in oral and written work. These materials require students to work in a communicative way, practising the use of English for different purposes, with encouragement and some guidance from the teacher.

These materials are flexible enough to be handled in a way different from that outlined above in diverse situations, depending on the constraints of the number of periods allotted per week in the time-table for the study of English, and their duration. This is possible because the materials have been designed primarily to help develop the linguistic skills of students and not to test their memory of the contents. Those in charge of the conduct of examinations will do well to bear this in mind.

Note to the teacher

As you will have realised from the Introduction, these materials require a teaching methodology which is quite different from the traditional 'lecture method'. At Anna University, we ourselves were using the lecture method until quite recently. In the lecture method the teacher is the centre of the class. The teacher talks whilst the students passively listen with varying degrees of attention. Thus only the teacher has the chance to practise spoken English for an extended period of time. But it is the students, of course, who need the practice. So it is felt that it will be more rewarding and enjoyable for all if the methodology is changed to a learner-centred one and the teacher assumes the role of guide and motivator.

Another problem with the lecture method is that it places considerable emphasis on the 'correct answers' to comprehension questions, to grammar exercises and to other written work. In other words the focus is on assessment of what students produce. But a teacher's job is not merely to assess but to promote learning. This is best done by shifting the focus to guiding the learning process through a series of carefully designed activities or tasks. We found the activities approach well-received by our students. In fact, one might characterise the professional activites of engineers and technologists as the solution of problems. So it is entirely appropriate and justifiable to use a problem-solving, task-based approach in the English classroom.

In this new approach, all the four skills involved in learning a language, namely reading, listening, speaking and writing are developed through various tasks. By working through the activities, students, both fluent and less fluent, should be able to improve their effectiveness in using English in real life situations especially for their chosen profession.

How to handle the main sections (Parts 1 and 2)

1. Reading tasks should be done by the students themselves, working in pairs or groups, or individually. You, the teacher, should resist any temptation to explain the whole text whilst the students read. Instead you should encourage the students to rely on their own resources and monitor their progress. When they have finished, the right answers can be arrrived at by discussion among students or at times you too can check the answers with the whole class.

2. Listening tasks are meant to give students practice in taking notes. You should therefore aim to give a talk using an informal lecture style. You should not read aloud from the 'Teacher's notes', but must prepare well in advance and present the information in the form of an informal lecture. This will require some skills, and even a little rehearsal on your part. But it allows for the listening material to be presented in a manner

suited to the ability of the students concerned. If the class has slow learners, speak more slowly with less complex grammar and with some repetition. With more accomplished students, you can make your mini-lecture more challenging. Whatever you do, do not read aloud from a prepared script ! Be natural and remember, spoken language is often less formal and certainly contains slips, false starts and hesitations, and these will be present in your mini-lecture, too.

3. Role-play, discussions and oral pair-work exercise should be made lively by encouraging each student to participate in the given task. You must not worry about the noise level in the classroom; indeed, the noise they make during these sessions indicates the degree of participation and involvement by the students in the given task.

4. Writing tasks must be closely monitored. The teacher should move among the students correcting their language. You should not wait for all of them to complete the whole task. Those who are slow in English should be closely monitored and more help can be given to them. Although you will naturally want to correct students' written work yourself, do not attempt to mark all their work yourself. Besides being far too burdensome, it is also bad training for your students. They should be encouraged to criticise, edit and correct their own work. In this way you can help them become mature, independent writers. Staff in other faculties will be grateful for your efforts.

Commenting on written work provides an opportunity for dealing differently with students of differing abilities. The weak student can perhaps be encouraged to produce work containing good ideas. Although accuracy of grammar and spelling are ultimately very important, correcting these mistakes too rigorously in the early stages will discourage your students. In any case, making mistakes is an important part of any learning process. When dealing with a more fluent student, on the other hand, you may want to point out even small mistakes so that he or she is encouraged to improve, and not to sit back, satisfied.

5. Language focus exercises should be done without the need for long explanations from you. As far as possible, grammatical labels should not be used. Your students' need is to be able to use English for their own purposes, and detailed grammatical analysis may not help them achieve this goal. Instead, use the language focus activities to develop your students' awareness of the language and how it works.

English teachers working with engineering and technology students are often apprehensive about dealing with anything related to engineering or technology in their classes, since their students are likely to know more than the teacher. However, with a communicative methodology, this can be exploited as a strength. Students are only too pleased to explain technical points to their English teacher, and other students will soon speak up if wrong information is given. These explanations provide samples of genuine communication and thus give excellent opportunities for students to practise oral communication. We have found that our students expect us to be experts in English, not in other subjects as well. Your experience is also likely to be similar. Thus a spirit of cooperation is created in the classroom, and this will benefit everyone.

Working with slow learners

Ideally, slow learners should be taught the Preparation and Follow-up materials in a separate special class. They should be able to follow the main materials in their regular class. In such special classes, particular attention should be paid to psychological aspects. The teacher should explain very carefully, in the mother-tongue if necessary, what the purpose of these 'extra' lessons is. They must be made to understand that these lessons are designed to increase their rate of learning so that they are not held back in their studies by their difficulty with English. Also, a lot of encouragement must be given to them whenever they attempt to complete a task, whether or not they make mistakes. Strict censorship and sarcastic comments must not be made at any stage or time, however wrong their response may seem to be. Fluency must be encouraged even at the cost of accuracy. Later on, they will slowly pick up accuracy too if they participate whole-heartedly without inhibitions. The teacher should always use simple language. It will be encouraging if the teacher holds back his or her own knowledge and even feigns ignorance so that the students feel compelled to use English to explain things, thus getting more practice in English.

Stretching abler students

Since this textbook aims at the development of the basic skills (LSRW) involved in language learning, those students who have already an excellent command of English may feel that these materials do not provide sufficient challenge. Such students' help may be effectively utilised by making them 'adopt' less able students and try to help them in completing their tasks. This will act as a morale booster for both the strong and the 'help-level' students. Also the tasks can be further stretched so that the creative ability of the stronger students in the use of language may be fully brought out. For example, they may be asked to collect supplementary materials connected with the topic from different sources including the library. They can play a leading role in tasks like discussion, oral practice and role-play, guiding the slow learner on the right lines so that at a later stage the special group may face these tasks independently with confidence and without external help.

It is never easy for teachers to change their methodology. By extended practice, it becomes a habit, and to deviate from that requires a lot of effort and conscious labour. We have tried using a communicative learner-centred appproach and found that we enjoy it. We want to encourage you to try this new methodology and we hope you too will enjoy it.

To the student

These materials, on different topics, have been prepared with you, the student, very much in mind. Students who have already tried out this book have found the topics interesting and useful. We hope you will also find them so. We believe that you can learn better if you are encouraged to join in discussions to solve problems and to express your ideas freely. These materials provide plenty of opportunities for you to take part in classroom activities of various kinds. The teachers will only guide and monitor you. You will often be asked to work with other students in pairs or in groups. In this way you can learn to speak English fluently and with confidence.

We have designed the main parts of each unit to enable you to read more efficiently. Practice in note-taking will help you with work in your other subjects too. Discussions and role-play will improve your fluency, and language focus exercises will deepen your understanding of how the English language works. All of these will help you to write better English in the writing tasks.

If you have difficulty in understanding English, you will find the Preparation and Follow-up sections in each unit very useful. The Preparation enables you to follow Parts 1 and 2 better. The Follow-up lesson helps you consolidate your learning from Parts 1 and 2. You need not hesitate to speak in English. Speak as much as you can. Do not worry too much about grammar, but try to make your meaning as clear as you can. Do not hesitate to ask your classmates or your teacher for help. If you do the various activities with genuine interest, you will definitely be benefitted by this course.

Whatever your level, this textbook encourages you to improve and polish your own English. If you are proficient in English, you can help your other classmates, encouraging them to participate in classroom activities and helping them to learn with you.

CONTENTS

Energy Unit 1

Oil

Preparation

OIL

1. Reading skills development

Look at the two columns A and B below quickly and match each statement in column B with a probable speaker from column A.

A	B
i. farmer	Petrol has become so expensive that many people prefer to use cheaper forms of transport.
ii. taxi driver	Frequent power cuts interfere with industrial production.
iii. housewife	Energised pump sets are a common feature of agricultural operations today.
iv. factory manager	Liquefied petroleum gas has made cooking easier.

2. Oral practice

a. Interview another student about his or her region. Begin your questions, like this :

Could you tell me something about your district ?
What about .... ?
Do you .... ?
How has .... developed in your ....?
Have there been many/any changes in ....?

b. Now imagine that you are going to interview a foreigner about his or her country.

Write as many questions as you can in the time given about the development, culture and way of life. Use the questions listed above if necessary.

3. Language development

a. Look at these examples of words with the prefixes **multi-** and **under-**.

A company with branches in many countries is called a multinational company.

A country which is not very highly developed is an underdeveloped country.

Now fill in the gaps in these sentences with words having the prefix **multi-** *or* **under-**.

i. A person with many millions of rupees is a ....

ii. A society whose people speak many languages is ....

iii. A child who does not have enough nourishment is ....

iv. An employed person who does not have enough work is ....

v. A building with many floors is a .... building

vi. When you think less of someone's abilities than the person actually has, you have .... him or her.

b. *Read the words in the box below. Note the stressed syllables.*

surfaces	exploit	oil-rich	feasible	conservation
feedstock	crude-oil	columns	lubrication	consumption

i. Many Arab countries are ....

ii. Petrol leaves the ground in the form of ....

iii. Friction is reduced by ....

iv. Bitumen or tar is used for road ....

v. Figures in log tables are arranged in horizontal rows and vertical ....

vi. Our .... of food must be limited to suit our digestive system.

vii. .... of energy will reduce demands for energy.

viii. Some greedy employers try to.............................. their employees.

ix. Before undertaking an adventurous project, one must consider whether it is .... or not.

x. Material which is fed into an industrial process is called ....

c. *Strike out the word that does not belong to the group. Say why it is different from the other words.*

For example: doctor, nurse, hospital, x-ray, nomad
Answer: All the other words are about health, but *nomad* is not.

i. economy, per capita income, wealth, treasure.

ii. industrial, rates of production, prices, dramatic, consumption.

iii. schools, deserts, universities, Mullah, colleges.

iv. swords, standstill, muskets, arms, weapons.

v. business, ransom, commodity, scarce, costly.

vi. tents, palaces, homes, camels.

If you are still unsure of any word, ask your teacher.

Part 1

1. **Discussion** —'The importance of energy'

Energy plays a major role in man's life. Whether it is for increasing agricultural production or for starting new industries, energy is extremely important.

Work in pairs. List situations where energy is important for development.

a. agricultural production b. .... c. ....
d. .... e. .... f. ....
g. .... h. ....

2. **Reading** — 'Interview with Sheik Sultan'

Many of the major oil-producing countries became rich almost overnight and as a result their societies changed dramatically.

a. Read this interview between a journalist and a seventy-year-old inhabitant of Shazanah, an imaginary oil-rich country. Sheik Sultan has seen many changes in his lifetime.

Journalist:	Salam Alaikum.
Sheik Sultan:	Alaikum salam.
Journalist:	First, can you tell me what your occupation is?
Sheik Sultan:	Well, now I own a few oil wells, factories and shops and have some interest in business too. But forty years ago, I was just a nomad in the desert.
Journalist:	What exactly do you mean?
Sheik Sultan:	Well, take food for example. In those days we had to hunt for food and water for days on end. Now I can have anything I want right away from the supermarket. We had to travel on foot or on a camel. These days everyone has a Cadillac or an Impala. We used to live in tents and be exposed to all kinds of weather conditions. Now we live in palaces and homes with air conditioning and every other luxury we want.

---

b. *Now read each of Sheik Sultan's answers and then fill in the question the journalist had asked.*

Journalist:	....?
Sheik Sultan:	Thanks to our oil, our country is very sound. We have the highest per capita income in the world and no one pays income tax.

Journalist: ....?

Sheik Sultan: We've opened a lot of schools and universities. You see, when I was young, I was taught only Arabic by a Mullah. I was just taught to read the Koran. But my sons have been educated at Harvard University in the USA.

Journalist: ....?

Sheik Sultan: We have the most modern hospitals. We have foreign specialists working in our hospitals. If need be, a patient can get treatment overseas and the State will pay the cost.

Journalist: ....?

Sheik Sultan: Well, there hasn't been much change here. Forty years ago, we had no industry. Now we are just beginning to develop some industries. Of course, most of the technicians are from other countries.

Journalist: ....?

Sheik Sultan: Well, we're very proud of our culture and our traditions. We are careful to preserve our traditions. Look — I'm still wearing traditional clothes, for example.

Journalist: ....?

Sheik Sultan: Well, I suppose I do, most of them. Inshah Allah, I do hope that we continue to prosper from our oil. But sometimes, you know, I long for the old days. Everyone has his nostalgic feelings.

Journalist: Well, Sheik Sultan, thank you for the interview. Goodbye.

Sheik Sultan: Khuda Hafiz. May God go with you.

---

c. **Now list the changes referred to in the journalist's interview with Sheik Sultan, and list the things which have not changed.**

d. **Can you think of any other questions you would like to ask Sheik Sultan?**

3. **Reading** — **'Oil and world economy'**

a. *Before you read the text, discuss these questions.*

i. **What do you understand by the term 'multinational'?**

ii. Can you name some multinational companies in India?

iii. What role do the multinational companies play in the world economy?

iv. What do you understand by the term 'oil-rich' countries?

v. Can you name some of these countries?

vi. What relationship do these countries have with the developed countries of the world?

b. Look at the text quickly and find out what and when the turning point was in the relationship between the developed countries and the oil-rich countries of the world.

Oil and World Economy

Oil, the major source of energy in the world today, has had a dramatic effect on the world's economy. Until quite recently, the demand for oil seemed unlimited. This enormous demand motivated several multinational companies to invest vast sums of money in locating and exploiting any large oil deposits that could be found. Some of these multinationals became extremely wealthy, although the countries in which they found oil did not always have much of a share in this new-found wealth.

However, oil-rich countries came to realise that if they acted together, their oil deposits could be a source of great power and wealth. Indeed, in 1973, the Organisation of Petroleum Exporting Countries (OPEC) which together produced 56 per cent of the world's petroleum at that time, decided to act together to force an increase in the price of oil. By united action, OPEC was able to take control of the rates of production and of prices away from the multinational companies. This action, by a group of developing countries almost held the developed world to ransom. Limiting the supply of oil led to sharp increases in what was becoming a scarce, though still vital, commodity. Without oil, the economies of the developed countries would have come to a virtual standstill. Almost overnight, there was a huge shift of wealth from industrial nations to the oil-exporting nations. Another effect was that industrialised countries became more interested in energy conservation. Indeed, by 1980, world oil consumption was down by 3 per cent on 1973 levels. A more long term effect was that other sources of energy which had previously been considered too costly now became economically feasible.

c. Look at this list of events. Look back at the text on page 52, and make two lists, one comprising those events which happened before 1973 and the other those events which happened after 1973.

i. Great increase of wealth in the oil-rich countries.
ii. Multinationals make huge investments in oil-rich countries.
iii. Industrialised countries attempt to conserve energy.
iv. Some increase of wealth in certain oil-rich countries.
v. Supply of oil to the world is limited.
vi. Great increase of wealth of some multinationals.
vii. Developed countries consider alternative energy sources.
viii. Oil prices increased dramatically.

Check your answers with a partner.

4. **Language focus** — 'Crude oil'

Correct the mistakes in the English in this passage.

OIL

One of the world's major source of energy are oil. We depend it for heating as fuel as well as transsport and generate power.

Crude mineral oil come out the earth as a thick brown or black liquid strong smelling. It is a complex mixture of many different substance, who have their own individual qualitys. Most of they is combinations of hydrogen and carbon in varying proportions. They contain various inpurities. So, crude oil necessary to refine before it can be used. The products obtained after refining used for different purpose.

Part 2

1. **Language focus** — 'Prospecting for oil'

   a. The sentences in the box below are not in the right sequence. Read each sentence and underline the reference words (it , they , etc.) .

   b. Number these jumbled sentences in the correct order to make a paragraph about prospecting for oil. Your answer to (a) should help.

   > - If that strikes oil, then production wells can be drilled.
   > - They carry out surveys from the ground and from the air using a variety of instruments, and they bore into the rocks to take samples.
   > - When petroleum engineers search for oil, they look for certain types of rock layers, or strata, which they know from past experience can trap oil.
   > - If it indicates that oil may be present, a test well is drilled.
   > - Oil is found underground trapped in the rock layers.
   > - When all the information is collected and analysed, a picture of the underground strata is obtained.
   > - They also set off explosions in the ground and record the waves reflected from the underground rock layers.
   > - This is called seismic surveying.

   c. Now decide what each of your underlined reference words actually refers to. Check your answers with your neighbour.

2. **Listening** — 'Oil refining'

   a. Listen to this short lecture and make notes. The framework below will help you. If you find listening very easy, make your own notes without looking at the framework.

Crude oil

a. Its physical properties
   i.
   ii.
   iii. can be fluorescent
   iv.

b. Its composition

c. Why it is refined

b. Before listening to the next section, check the notes you and your neighbour have. Do you have the same points ?

The oil refining process

a. Process employed to separate out different hydrocarbons

b. Principle on which the separation takes place

c. How an oil distillation plant functions :

.... fractionating columns
feedstock ....
....

Now check your notes.

c. *Products of distillation*

column level	name of product (fraction)	products used as or for
top	a. b. c.	(after blending)
middle	a. b.	(after blending)
bottom	(tar)	

Now check your notes.

d. *Processes to improve yield*

name of process	feedstock used	achievements of process
a.		
b.		

Now check your notes.

3. **Discussion** — ' A world without oil '

What would the world be like if our supplies of oil were to run out (or become unobtainable) ?

a. Make a list of all the things you can think of which come from crude oil, not forgetting products of the petro-chemical industries.

b. Classify the uses of your listed items using general headings such as 'domestic', 'industrial', 'transportation', 'chemical'.

4. **Writing** — 'A world without oil'

Imagine it is now fifty years in the future. There is no oil left. Write a paragraph telling your grandchildren how life was better, because of oil, in the twentieth century. Begin :

> In my day, oil was plentiful, we could .... but these days we cannot ....

Follow-up

1. **Language check**

To check your understanding of some of the words in the last two lessons, tick the word or phrase on the right which is nearest in meaning to the word on the left. *Turn to page* 12

a.	*invest*	introduce; change; lay out money for profit
b.	*vast*	very large; garment; unnecessary
c.	*ransom*	beautiful; running fast; a sum of money
d.	*exploit*	extract; explore; make gain out of
e.	*deposits*	depot; posts; accumulation
f.	*vital*	very tall; very important; very old
g.	*shift*	garment; move; dig

2. Language development

a. *Look at the following comparative adjectives and put them into four groups according to how they are formed :*

larger
wealthier
more powerful
more efficient
more interested
heavier
better
bigger
easier
more important
worse
greater
cheaper
higher
more traditional
wetter

b. *Write the comparative forms of the following adjectives :*

dry
valuable
greedy
good
professional
rare
sturdy
simple
feasible
beautiful
reliable
pure

3. Reading skills development

a. *Read the passage and fill in the middle column of the chart which follows it.*

Coal is a hydrocarbon deposit which is mined either manually or mechanically. It is found in layers beneath the ground, the deeper layers generally providing the better coal. Coal is almost always hard, opaque (non-transparent) and black. Of all the primary fossil fuels, coal has by far the greatest reserves and is found in many countries. Besides being burnt directly to provide heat energy, coal is also an important source of gas and chemicals. Amongst other things, coal can be used to produce detergents, explosives, drugs, paints, lubricants, motor spirit and food. Like oil-based proteins, though, proteins from coal have a strange taste and are used for feeding animals.

	COAL	OIL
easily available?		
where found?		
what is it?		
what does it look like?		
how is it extracted?		
uses before processing?		
end-products after processing?		

b. **Now fill in the last column of the chart above.**

4. Oral practice

Work in pairs. Use the chart above to ask and answer questions about coal and oil, like this :

> **Is coal easily available ?**
> **Where is oil found ?**

5. **Writing skills development**

Using the chart above, write a paragraph comparing coal and oil. Follow the order of the chart, writing one sentence for each line of the chart. Try to use these phrases :

Unlike oil, coal ....

In contrast to oil, coal ....

Coal is .... whereas oil is ....

Like oil, coal is ....

Coal and oil are both ....

Energy Unit 2

Nuclear power

NUCLEAR POWER

Preparation

1. **Oral practice**

   a. What do you understand by the term 'nuclear energy'?

   b. Are there any dangers in the use of nuclear energy?

   c. Do you know of any accidents involving nuclear energy?

2. **Language development**

   a. Look at the words in column A and make sure you can pronounce them properly.

   b. For each word in column A, find its meaning in column B.

A	B
nucleus	division of the atom
uranium	getting rid of
fission	pollution
disposal	central part of the atom
core	producer
coolant	metallic element
breeder	giving out rays
radiation	danger
hazard	cooling fluid
contamination	the innermost part

   c. Can you guess the meanings of these words and phrases (if you do not know them already)?

derived from	consumption	generated by
depleted	disaster	abuse

Now fill in the blanks in the sentences below with these words and phrases.

i. In hydel units, electricity is .... heating water.

ii. Vast quantities of energy can be .... a very small quantity of nuclear fuel.

iii. Th existing coal reserves will fast become .... if we continue to use such a large amount of coal.

iv. Our present .... of oil and gas exceeds the present production levels.

v. An accident in a nuclear power station can lead to a great ....

vi. Causing destruction through atom bombs is a clear example of .... of scientific knowledge.

3. Language development

Use the appropriate form of the adjectives in the box to complete the following sentences.

easy	valuable	radioactive
difficult	renewable	expensive
	costly	

a. LPG has made cooking ....

b. Petrol is .... kerosene.

c. .... energy sources include the sun, wind and water.

d. When oil becomes ...., many countries consider using alternative energy sources for economic reasons.

e. Uranium and plutonium are .... nuclear fuels.

f. Some refined products of crude oil are .... than others.

g. Prospecting for oil is, in many ways, ... than extracting it.

4. Oral practice

Look at this diagram of a nuclear reactor.

Can you guess what the numbered parts are?

Do you know how the reactor works? Is the diagram correct?

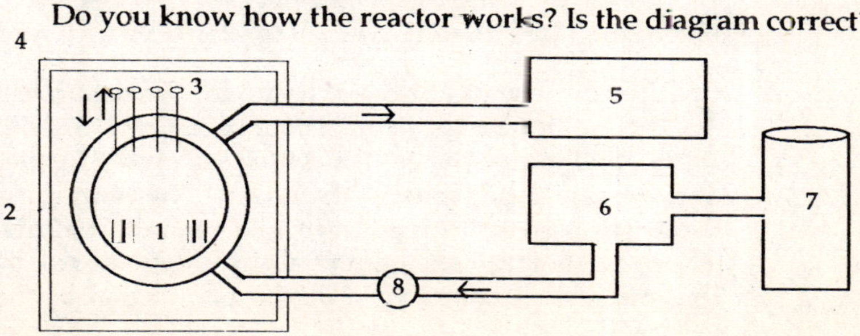

Part 1

NUCLEAR POWER

1. **Reading** — 'Why India needs nuclear power'

   a. i. What does 'energy' mean to people in India?
   Think of three people from different walks of life.
   How would they respond to this question?

   What do you know about nuclear power?

   ii. Why do you think it is called this?
   What do you know about nuclear fuels?

   iii. This reading text is about the reasons for India to develop nuclear power. What do you think the reasons may be? Make a list.

   b. i. Reading the first sentence only of a paragraph can often give you an idea of what the whole paragraph is about. Try out this technique on the four paragraphs below, making a note of what you think each paragraph is about

   ii. Which part of the text tells you the reasons why India is developing nuclear power? Reading this part only, compare the reasons given with the reasons on the list you made earlier in (a) iii above.

Reasons for India to Develop Nuclear Power

A. Coal-fired thermal units and hydel units are at present the major sources of electric power generation in India. Sixtythree per cent of it is based on the former and thirtyfour per cent on the latter. The remaining three per cent is derived from nuclear power units. The capacity for power generation is likely to go up by the end of this century. But the population of the country is also expected to increase considerably by then. The power available will be sufficient to meet only about sixty per cent of the minimum requirement.

B. The country's coal resources amount to about 112 billion tonnes. The rate of coal raising is likely to go up from the present 155 million tonnes to 400 million tonnes by the year 2000. Assuming that only fifty per cent of the coal reserves in the ground can be recovered, these will be depleted in about 125 years. Moreover, the ash in Indian coal is highly abrasive and this poses serious problems to power plant equipment. Coal prices are also fast rising. It is felt that burning coal for power generation leads to environmental hazards like acid rain.

C. There is, thus, a need for a gradual shift from coal to other energy sources. However, hydel power generation is becoming increasingly difficult as it involves submergence of valuable forest areas and the rehabilitation of large populations. The present level of production of oil and gas is about two thirds of the present consumption. This cannot be maintained probably beyond fifteen years. Alternative sources of energy such as solar, wind and biogas can only have limited applicability.

D. Thus a new form of energy has to be developed in a big way. Nuclear power can very well be the solution. The existing uranium reserves in the country can support a pressurised heavy water reactor programme. Similarly, the thorium reserves can be used in fast breeder reactors. A very small quantity of nuclear fuel can produce energy that can be produced only by vast quantities of conventional fuel like coal.

c. Work in pairs. Read one paragraph. Think of a heading for it in consultation with your partner. If you finish quickly, choose another paragraph for the same purpose. Be ready to report back when the teacher asks you to do so.

d. Work in pairs. Write down two or three words you are not familiar with which you think are important in the paragraph (s) you have just read. Try to guess their meanings in consultation with your partner. Later, your teacher will write the words the class does not know on the board. The teacher will explain the meaning of some of the important words.

2. **Listening** — ' Two kinds of nuclear reactor'

You are going to listen to a short talk about two types of nuclear reactor. Use the framework below to help you.

	1	2
type of reactor		
reason for name		
coolant system		
relative merits		
other information		

3. **Discussion** — 'Which nuclear reactor?'

Using the notes you have just taken, decide which type of nuclear reactor you would recommend, and make out a case. Then defend your choice to your partner. (For a better discussion, don't choose the same reactor as your partner!)

4. **Reading**

a. The diagram below shows the main parts of a typical nuclear reactor.
Can you guess the name or function of any of these parts?

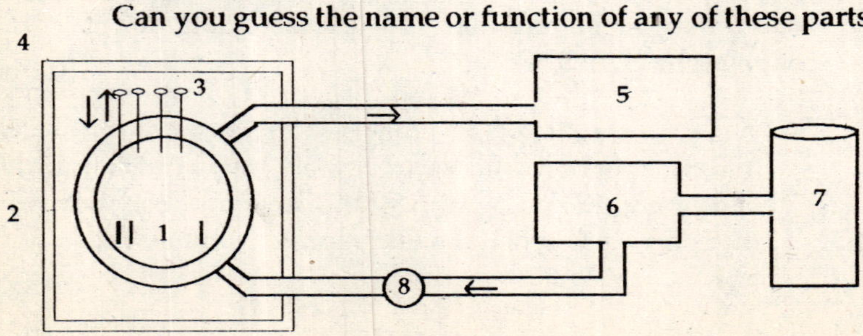

b. Now read the text and write down the correct names of the parts.
Check with your neighbour.

Layout of a Typical Nuclear Reactor

The uranium fuel is contained in the reactor's core. The reactor is controlled by control rods which can be driven into and out of the core. The core is usually enclosed in a pressure vessel which is surrounded by a biological shield. This is a concrete structure designed to prevent the escape of radiation from the core. The reactor heats the water which is circulated and converted directly or indirectly to steam. The steam drives a turbine generator which produces energy in the ordinary way. Exhaust steam is converted back into water by means of a condenser which uses water from a cooling tower. The cooling tower needs a supply of cold water from a river or the sea. The cold water is circulated by a feedwater pump back through the hot part of the reactor.

c. If you have extra time, make a note of the function of each part.

1 ....

2 ....

3 ....

4 ....

5 ....

6 ....

7 ....

8 ....

Part 2

NUCLEAR POWER

1. **Reading** — 'Dangers and disasters'

   a. *Make brief notes to answer these questions*

      i. What dangers do you think can arise from the use of nuclear power?

      ii. Can you think of any possible abuse of nuclear power?

      iii. What instances can you recall of a disaster involving nuclear power?

      iv. What safety measures do you think should be adopted while dealing with nuclear power?

   b. *Now skim the text entitled below quickly and suggest a suitable heading for each paragraph.*

Dangers and Disasters

....

Nuclear fuels such as uranium and plutonium are radioactive. They give out dangerous and very penetrative radiation. During fission even more radiation is produced. This radiation is harmful even in small quantities. It attacks living tissues and it can alter the genes in body cells. Such mutation can affect later generations. In large quantities its effect is lethal.

....

Nuclear reactors produce wastes which remain dangerously radioactive for hundreds or perhaps thousands of years. The disposal of these wastes is a serious problem. At present, they are often stored in underground tanks or sealed in containers and dropped into deep ocean trenches. Neither method is very satisfactory. The threat of environmental pollution is always there.

....

Nuclear plants need to be suitably located away from densely populated areas. Adequate waste disposal facilities must be available. The reactor ought to be surrounded by concrete and steel walls thick enough to prevent any escape of radiation. The working of the reactor should be slowed down by inserting control rods, also known as neutron absorbing rods, into the core. It is necessary that the reactor has emergency systems to cope with any unexpected failure of the fuel elements of the cooling system. Workers at the plants must protect themselves against possible contamination by using gloves, overshoes, respirators etc. Radiation measuring instruments have to be used to monitor radiation levels in and around the plants. It should be ensured that all releases into air and water are kept well below permissible levels.

---

c. Does the text answer all the questions in (a) above?

2. **Language focus** — 'Safety in nuclear plants'

a. Underline all the phrases in the third paragraph of the text above which express recommendations (e.g. It should be ensured that .....).

b. Work in pairs. Using the expressions you have just underlined, ask and anwer questions about safety measures in nuclear power plants.

3. **Reading** — 'Chernobyl'

The text below, from *The Hindu Survey of Indian Industry 1986*, describes the accident which took place at the Chernobyl nuclear plant in the Soviet Union.

a. Skim the text for gist. (1 minute)

b. Read the text quickly, noting which sections discuss the main factors contributing to the disaster.

c. Make notes about these factors under the headings *design*, *staffing* and *procedures*.

There are more than 350 nuclear power reactors in the world and no loss of life has been caused by their operation. Unfortunately, a reactor accident in April 1986 to Unit-4 of the Chernobyl plant has resulted in the loss of lives, contamination of the environment around the plant site and radioactive releases into the atmosphere. The loss of life was confined to certain plant per-

sonnel and those that were part of the emergency response crews, and has not extended to members of the public.

There are major differences between the Chernobyl reactor and the Indian pressurised heavy water reactors. The Chernobyl reactor was graphite moderated and water cooled. Hot graphite and water make a dangerous combination if they come into contact as large amounts of hydrogen are produced. When the fuel was starved of cooling, rupture of the pressure tubes leading to graphite-water reaction took place. The graphite caught fire on contact with air after the explosion. No graphite is used in Indian reactors. The Chernobyl plant was housed in an industrial type of building and the upper part of the reactor did not have proper containment provisions. The situation in India is different since it is one of the few countries which have adopted the use of the double containment principle for all its reactors designed from the mid-seventies onwards.

At Chernobyl, the accident occurred while the operators were carrying out a test on the turbogenerator with improper test procedures from the safety point of view and in serious violation of basic operating rules. No less than seven specific violations took place. In addition, being an early generation design, more reliance was placed on manual intervention for ensuring reactor safety than is customary with present day designs.

It is significant that both the Three Mile Island and the Chernobyl accidents took place at a time when plant operators were in charge, while in India graduate engineers with adequate training are in charge of the stations at all times.

> **Learner awareness**
> What you have been doing is a form of study reading which is useful when you have a clear purpose for your reading.

4. **Writing** — 'Chernobyl'

Using the notes made under 3 (c) above, write a paragraph about the main factors contributing to the disaster. Then, write a list of recommendations for ensuring safety in nuclear plants in the future.

NUCLEAR POWER

Follow-up

1. **Oral practice**

Work in pairs. Look back to the diagram of a nuclear reactor on page 17 Ask and answer questions about the parts of the reactor and their functions, like this:

Where is the ....?
What is this called?
What is the function of this?
What is the purpose of the .....?

Try to answer your partner's questions as quickly and clearly as you can.

2. **Comprehension check**

Look back at the text 'Why India Needs Nuclear Power' on page 18 and say whether these statements are true or false. Correct the false statements.

a. Thirtyfour per cent of electric power generated is derived from coal-fired thermal units.

b. The amount of power generated will decrease by the year 2000 A.D.

c. It may be possible to recover only 50 per cent of the stocks of coal in the ground.

d. Indian coal is suitable for use in power plant equipment.

e. Burning coal pollutes the atmosphere.

f. There are problems in hydro-electric generation.

g. Nuclear energy has been developed in a big way.

h. Large quantities of coal will be needed to produce the energy that can be produced by a small quantity of uranium.

3. **Language check**

Fill in the blank spaces in the box with the appropriate form of the word.

verb	noun	adjective
generate	....	generative
....	derivation	derivative
require	....	required
develop	development	....
penetrate	penetration	....
dispose	....	disposable
....	recovery	recoverable
....	depletion	depleted

4. **Language check**

Your teacher will dictate a short passage to you from this week's lessons. Write down what is said and then look back to the relevant lesson and check your spelling, grammar and punctuation.

5. Writing skills development

Use the notes you made from the listening exercise on page 20 to complete this paragraph comparing the two types of nuclear reactor.

One of the main differences between the pressurised heavy water reactor and the fast breeder reactor is that the PHW uses water as a coolant while the fast breeder reactor uses liquid sodium metal for this purpose.

Also, ... smaller ....

Therefore, ... more compact ....

.... higher power density ....

.... lower capital costs.......................................

.. more common ....

But, ... more efficient ....

... twice as much ....

Energy Unit 3

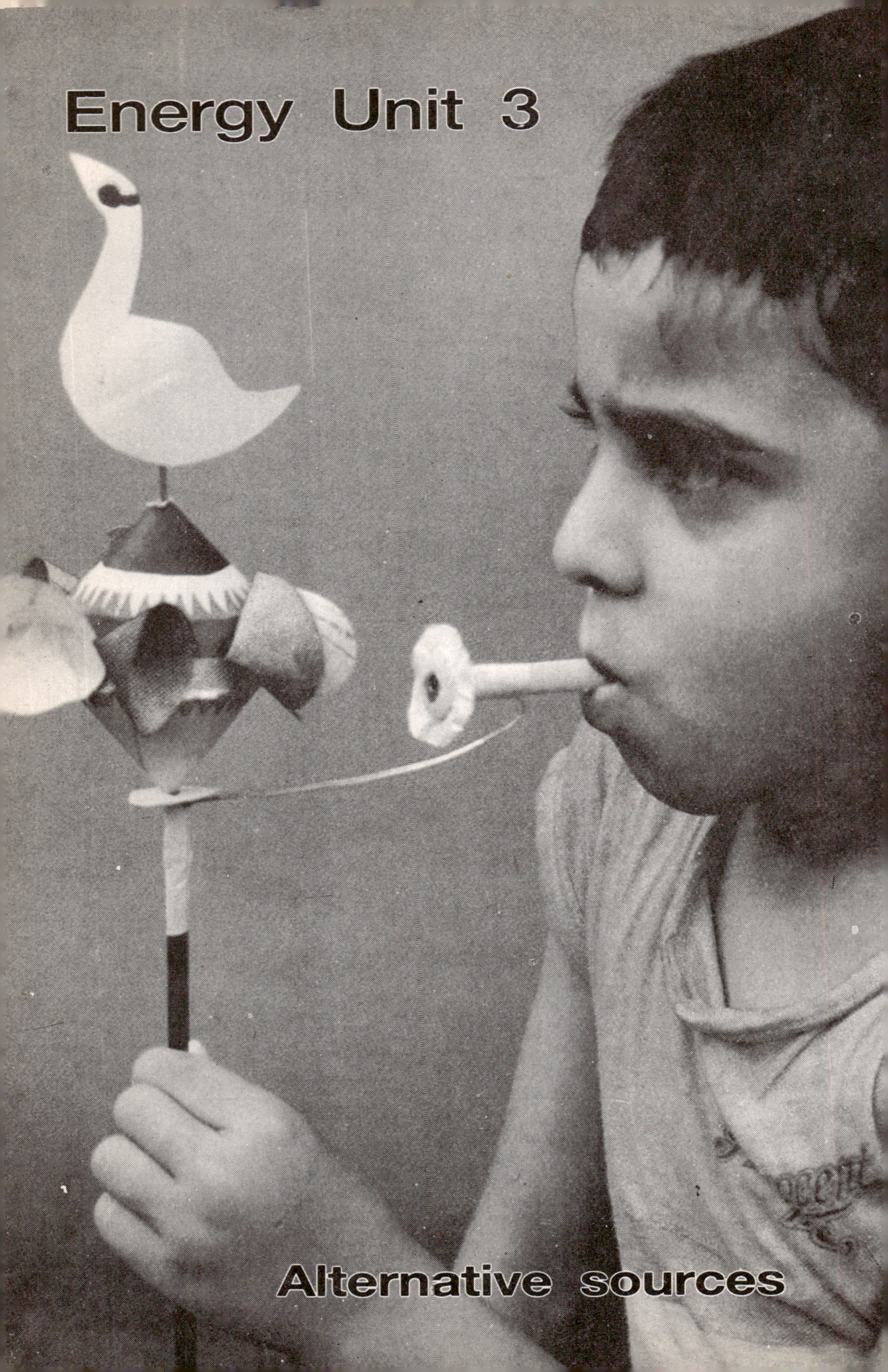

Alternative sources

ALTERNATIVE ENERGY SOURCES

Preparation

1. Language development

a. *Choose suitable words from the box to fill in the gaps in this passage. Use each word only once.*

renewable	fuel	commercial	needs
	source	population	alternative
	natural	facilitate	demand

Coal was the most widely used .... until the middle of the twentieth century. Since the 1950's the use of coal has declined rapidly and oil and natural gas serve as the main .... of energy these days. In the last sixty years, the world's energy .... have increased by 800 per cent and they are likely to increase further. Since the .... fuels such as oil and gas will run out during the next fifty years, we have to discover new ways of getting the energy we need.

One of the main reasons for the increase in the .... for energy fuel in a developing country like India is the enormous growth in .... Most of the people here live in villages where the .... sources of energy are found in plenty. They can be trained to make use of these. For example, biomass, the sun, animal waste, wind and water can all serve as .... sources of energy. Unlike the commercial fuels, they are .... because they can never be exhausted. Various systems and devices have been introduced to .... the use of these renewable sources of energy, none of which causes environmental pollution.

b. i. *For each word in column A find a word in column B with the opposite meaning.*

A	B
abundant	simple
artificial	desalination
former	natural

sophisticated latter
salination limited

Learn the correct pronunciation of these words with your teacher's help.

ii. *Now fill in one of the words above in each of these gaps.*

a. Since the reserves of oil and .... gas are .... we have to look for other energy sources.

b. The developed countries should help the developing countries so that the .... can meet the basic necessities of their people.

c. The gobar gas plant, or bio-gas generator, is a .... apparatus when compared to a nuclear reactor, which is far more ....

d. In spite of the higher cost involved in the process of ...., it is used on a large scale in many oil-producing countries because there is an acute shortage of water there.

2. Oral practice

Read the text on page 29 again. Now tick (✓) those items on the list below that you consider to be the advantages of alternative sources of energy.

causes atmospheric pollution	easily available
renewable	less expensive
involves high technology	can be quickly exhausted

Compare your list with another student's.
Now say which of the advantages of using alternative sources of energy make it appropriate for India. Offer examples to support your opinion.

Be ready to say what you think when your teacher asks you.

3. Language development

a. Make nouns of the following verbs by adding the suffix *-tion*, e.g. salinate — salination.

construct	pollute	conserve	destroy
compose	electrify	irrigate	ferment

b. Make as many words as you can from the following by adding different endings.

Check that you know the meanings of all the words.
Be ready to put them in sentences to show their meaning when your teacher asks you.

e.g. science .... scientific, scientist

i. photo ....

ii. maintain ....

iii. alternate ....

iv. renew ....

v. inferior ....

ALTERNATIVE ENERGY SOURCES

Part 1

1. **Language focus** — ' Alternative energy sources '

a. *Complete the text below by selecting the most appropriate word or phrase from the alternatives given in the right-hand column.*

The use of alternative .... sources of	*artificial / natural*
energy is attractive because of the high price and .... availabi-	*abundant/ limited*
lity of oil, the pollution that is associated with the burning of fossil fuels, the	

tremendous expense and .... of nuclear power, and a variety of other reasons.	*dangers/ users*
In .... countries, their initial development came at a time of relatively plentiful oil supplies at .... cost. This resulted in their	*developing/ developed* *lower/ higher*
being more .... this single source of energy than is true	*independent of/ reliant on*
in the .... countries.	*developing/ developed*

b. Check your answers with a partner before your teacher checks with the class.

2. **Discussion** — ' Drawbacks of electricity '

a. Working in pairs, list the problems involved in producing and using electricity in India.

b. Continue to work in pairs. Read each of the following statements and decide if you think they are true or false. State your reasons.

i. Alternative natural sources of energy are so cheap, there is no need to use them carefully.

ii. There are only three renewable sources of energy.

iii. Energy conservation is cheaper than extra energy production.

iv. Alternative sources of energy involve little or no environmental pollution or destruction.

v. These alternative energy technologies are relatively simple in construction and maintenance.

vi. Alternative energy technologies have a stigma of technical inferiority since they are applicable only to small scale industries.

vii. The power needs of larger industries can be met by alternative energy units.

viii. Energy from natural sources is not sufficient to meet the fuel needs of the rural masses in India.

3. **Reading — ' Two alternative energy devices '**

a. Below are descriptions of two alternative energy devices. One is used in a developing country, the Philippines, and the other was in common use in a developed country, the United States.
After reading the passages you will be asked to choose the device you feel would be more suitable for use in India.

A. **Pedal power**

Pedalling is probably the most efficient use of the muscles of the human body. Pedal power, using either a bicycle-like pedal arrangement or a treadle mechanism, can be used to power a variety of agricultural equipment, water pumps, grinders and electric generators.

At the International Rice Research Institute in the Philippines, engineers have developed a small, lightweight, inexpensive foot-powered pump that will lift large quantities of water several feet, using only moderate amounts of human power. The operator simply stands on two footrests at either end of the pump and rocks back and forth. This effect compresses a diaphragm which forces water from the outlet valve. By operating the pump in a rhythmic manner, a continuous flow of water is pumped.

B. **Wind power**

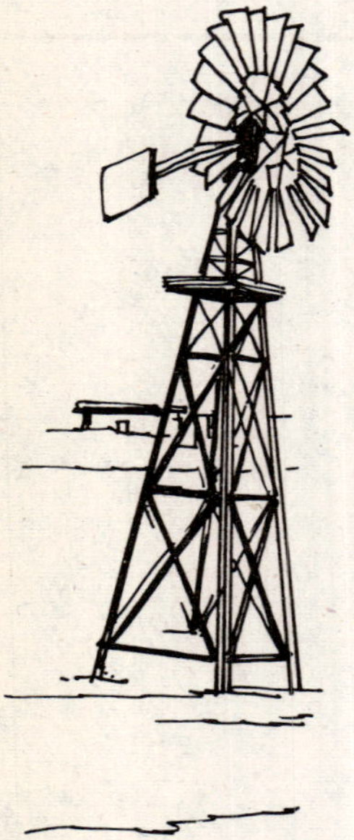

Wind energy has been used for thousands of years to propel boats and ships. Traditionally, the rural population in the USA used windmills principally for the following applications:

a. to pump water for domestic use and for watering livestock and irrigating crops;

b. to perform agricultural tasks such as grinding corn, threshing, cutting sugarcane, and wood-cutting;

c. for special applications such as moving saline water in salt works;

d. for the generation of electricity.

Before rural electrification, there were dozens of manufacturers of wind-powered pumps and electric generators in the United States. Today, however, it seems that only two continue to make windmills, and both manufacture the typical multiblade 'American' fan wheel. These pumps are primarily used on very large cattle farms in the West to provide water for livestock. They make use of a reciprocating cylinder pump that will deliver upto several hundred gallons per hour, depending on the depth of the well, the diameter of the pump cylinder and velocity of the wind.

b. ***Fill in this chart with information from the texts you have just read.***

	pedal power	**windmill**
resources needed		

machinery needed		
possible uses		

4. **Writing** — ' A device for rural India '

   a. *Consider both pedal and wind power in the context of rural India. Fill in this chart to help you compare their relative merits.*

in rural India	pedal power	windmill
necessary resources available?		
necessary machinery available?		
machinery sufficiently familiar?		
local construction possible?		
maintenance simple enough?		
uses required?		

Now using this chart, write a paragraph explaining which of these devices would be more suitable for use in rural India. Plan your paragraph with the help of the chart.

Part 2

1. **Discussion** — ' Energy for cooking'

   In pairs, decide what energy source might be used for cooking in the following places.

   a five-star hotel
   a houseboat in Kashmir
   a village hotel
   an open-air tea shop
   a mountain region
   an apartment in New York
   an industrial canteen

2. **Reading** — ' Bio-gas plants'

   a. *Take a quick glance (one minute only) at the following passage in six parts and then decide whether it comes from*

      a. an advertisement,
      b. a government handbook, or
      c. a novel.

   b. The six headings here come from the passage. Match each one with the relevant section of the passage. The sections are numbered for your convenience. After completing this task, check your answers with a partner.

      Two Main Products of Bio-gas Plants and their Uses

      What is Bio-gas?

      The Development of the Gobar Gas Plant

      What is the Gobar Gas Plant?

      Harnessing Renewable Sources of Energy

      Alternative Fuels for the Gobar Plant

i. To meet the growing needs of the increasing population, the agricultural productivity of land will have to be increased, requiring more inputs of energy and more fertilizers. Meeting these and other energy needs from conventional sources proves increasingly difficult and costly. The right way to meet this energy crisis is by finding ways to harness the renewable sources of energy which are locally available in rural areas. These renewable sources like bio-mass, animal wastes, wind and water will serve as alternatives to commercial fuels like coal, oil and electricity. They are non-polluting and also help to preserve the environment. They can be the cheapest sources of energy and a combination of these with solar energy systems can provide not only the most desirable but, in fact, the most economical option. Research development and demonstration projects have generated a variety of devices and systems for exploiting renewable energy sources: wind pumps, solar thermal systems, high efficiency smokeless furnaces, bio-gas plants and many more.

ii. The gobar gas plant, or bio-gas generator, is a simple apparatus for turning animal dung into bio-gas plus nitrogen fertiliser. Gobar comes from the Hindi word for cow. Cattle dung forms the primary source of fuel for the rural population in India.

iii. As early as 1939, in India the gobar gas plant was developed on an experimental basis. This was followed by the installation of a commercial model in 1954. In 1962 the Khadi and Village Industries Commission (KVIC) adopted the bio-gas/gobar gas programme and took initiative to install a number of bio-gas plants in various places in India.

iv. Bio-gas is a gas mixture containing about 60 per cent methane, a high value fuel, and 40 per cent carbondioxide, an inert gas, plus traces of other gases such as nitrogen and hydrogen sulphide obtained from anaerobic (without oxygen) fermentation of dung in the presence of micro-organisms.

v. Wherever the availability of cattle dung is found to be inadequate, the same can be supplemented with other materials. The other supplementary materials are human excreta, pig dung and poultry droppings, organic wastes, water hyacinth, corn stalks, wild grass, aquatic weeds, and so on. The mixing of equal parts of animal dung, water hyacinth and algae results in a high proportion of methane, up to 70 per cent. A one-acre plot of water hyacinth would yield 1100 cu ft of gas per day or 400,000 cu ft/yr which is equivalent to 60 MW power.

vi. The two main products from bio-gas plants are bio-gas and processed slurry (manure). Bio-gas can be used as a fuel for domestic cooking or for running diesel engines. Processed slurry leaving a bio-gas plant is rich in nitrogen, phosphorus and potassium and humus. The precise composition varies from place to place. It can be most profitably applied to the soil directly or after mixing with irrigation water.

c. Now read parts of the passage again more carefully in order to answer the following questions. Use the headings to help you find the relevant part of the passage for each question.

i. What is the fundamental cause of the energy crisis?
ii. Suggest two ways of making use of renewable sources of energy.
iii. Why is the bio-gas production system of greater value than the simple burning of organic waste or dung?

v. What other materials can be used in a bio-gas plant when there is a shortage of animal wastes?

vi. What is meant by anaerobic fermentation?

3. **Role play** — 'Renewable energy sources'

Student A : You are a foreign journalist visiting India. You want to know about the use of alternative energy sources in India. Prepare a list of questions to ask the Secretary, Department of Non-conventional Energy Sources, Government of India.

Student B : You are the Secretary, Department of Non-conventional Energy Sources, Government of India. You will be interviewed by a foreign journalist on the use of renewable energy sources in India. Be prepared to answer his/her questions.

Start when you are both ready. Try to keep the interview quite formal.

4. **Writing** — ' Energy for India '

Choose *one* form of energy which you consider to be suitable for further development in India. You may look back at the last three weeks of work for ideas. Write three short paragraphs in the way described below.

paragraph 1 : Introduce India's energy needs .

paragraph 2 : Compare your choice with other alternatives.

paragraph 3 : Summarise the advantages of your chosen form of energy.

Follow-up

1. **Comprehension check**

   a. Before your teacher talks to you about pedal power, read these sentences below.

      i. Pedal power can only be used for one type of agricultural equipment.
      ii. The foot-powered pump developed in the Philippines will lift large quantities of water.
      iii. This pump needs a great amount of human power.
      iv. It does not weigh very much but it is expensive.
      v. It is not possible to pump a continuous flow of water using this pump.

   b. Now listen to your teacher and decide if the sentences are true or false.

2. **Language check**

   Your teacher will dictate a passage to you about wind power. Check your spelling and punctuation carefully with reference to the text on page 34

3. **Oral practice**

   a. Using the chart you prepared on page 35 ask and answer questions. Work with another student.

   b. Say which of these devices would be more suitable for use in rural India. State your reasons. Try to make use of appropriate comparative adjectives.

4. **Language check**

   Read the following passage through , then try to fill in the missing words.

   These .... sources like biomass, animal .... wind and water will serve as

.... to commercial ....
like coal, oil and electricity. They are non-polluting and also help to preserve the .... Research development and demonstration projects have generated a variety of devices and systems for exploiting renewable energy
.... : wind.................................... ,
.... thermal systems, high efficiency
.... furnaces, bio-gas ....
and many more.

Check your answers with another student, then look back at the text on page 37 and check.

Computers Unit 1

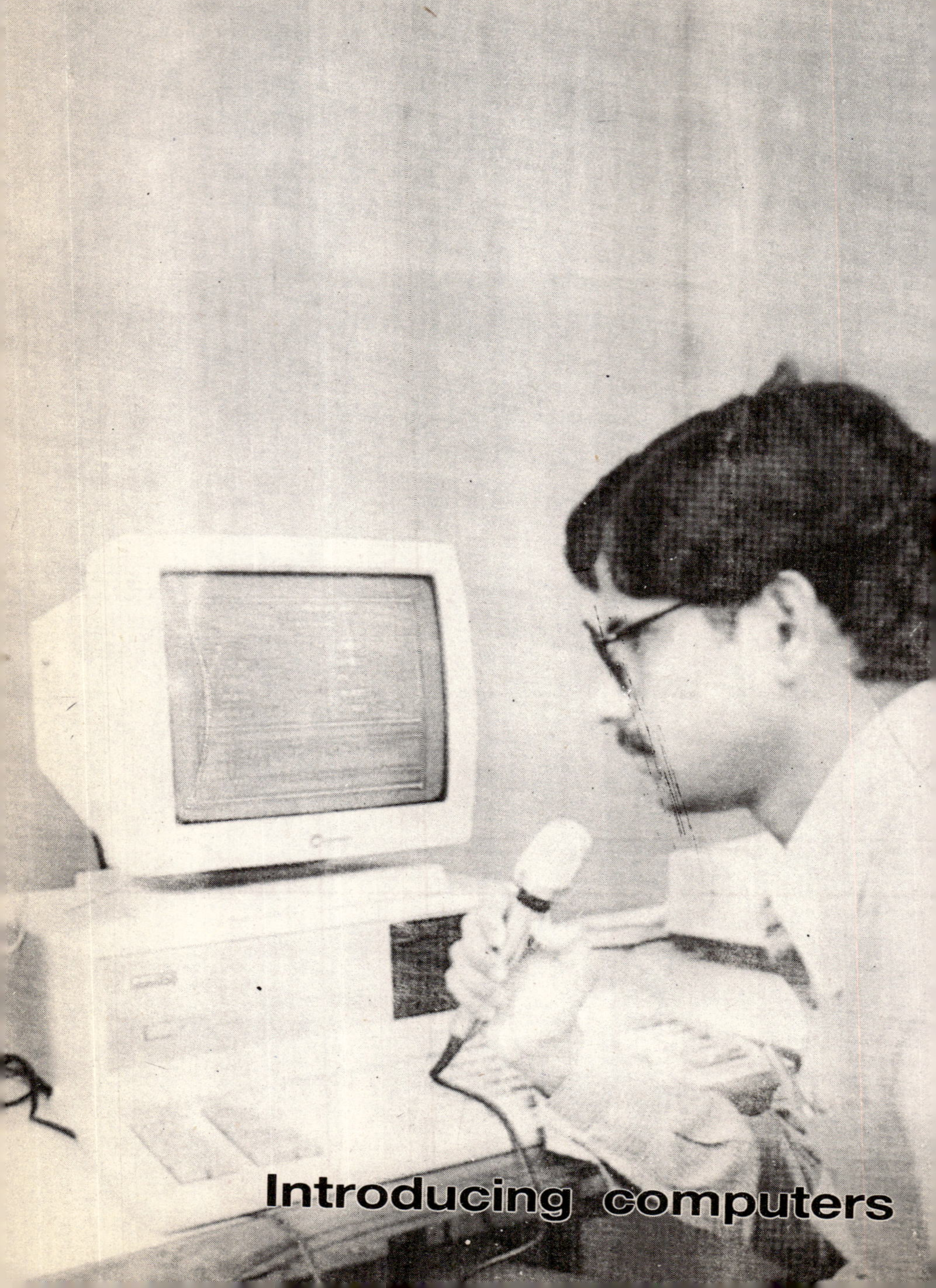

Introducing computers

Preparation

INTRODUCING COMPUTERS

1. Language development

In any science, it is vital to be precise about terminology. Definitions of key terms are needed. Decide which of the following are definitions, and which are not.

a. A laboratory is a room which is used for experimenting.

b. A computer is an expensive machine.

c. A calculator is a machine which can perform arithmetical and some other logical operations.

d. Mathematics is a very ancient subject.

e. Petroleum is a fuel used by motor engines such as buses and cars.

f. A computer program is a set of instructions which tells a computer what to do.

A good definition should be precise, and it should identify the thing you are defining beyond any doubt. For example, in (b) above, 'an expensive machine' could be a car, a space rocket or many other things. Show by example what is wrong with the other non-definitions above.

Now try to write definitions of an abacus, log tables, a typewriter and an audio-cassette tape. Use the pattern 'x is a y which ...'

2. Language development

a. *Try to guess the meanings of the words in capital letters by looking at the examples.*

SCREEN	a cinema screen, a TV screen
SOURCE	an energy source, the source of the Ganges, the source of the problem
CAPACITY	a one-litre capacity bottle, capacity of bus: 70 passengers

DEVICE — a measuring device, a device for heating food, a balancing device

DISPLAY — food on display in a market, an aeronautics display, a display of skill

MEMORY — a memory like an elephant, a calculator with a memory, a short memory

POWER — electric power, nuclear power, wind power, political power

Make sure you can pronounce all these words correctly. Your teacher will help.

b. English can make compound nouns by putting two suitable nouns together:

POWER SOURCE — a source of power

ARITHMETIC UNIT — a unit in which arithmetic is performed

MAINS ELECTRICITY — electricity which comes from the mains

In pairs, explain: energy source; control centre; cassette tape; calculator memory; calculation speed; video screen.

c. *Fill in each gap with a simple or compound noun from those you have been studying.*

The modern calculator can use either batteries or .... as its .... Its .... is becoming even faster, and long repetitive calculations are made possible by a .... Input is through the use of keys, and output is displayed on a small ....

3. Oral practice

a. When you compare two things, you do so on the basis of features, or parameters applicable to both. Thus, you may compare a man with an elephant on the basis of *weight* or *life-span* and say that, for instance,

the elephant is heavier than a man

the elephant lives longer than a man

Suppose you want to compare logarithm tables with a pocket calculator. With your partner, first decide on some features you want to compare, such as *cost* or *energy source*. Once you have atleast three more items, draw a table, like this:

	log tables	calculator
cost		
energy source		

and fill in all the boxes.

b. *Using the table, compare log tables with calculators, like this.*

A: What about an energy source?

B: Well, log tables ...., but calculators ....

When you practise, try hard to be accurate in your English and to be fluent!

4. Writing skills development

a. The words *but, however, whereas* and *while* have something in common. What is it?

Decide whether each of these words can be used :

i. at the beginning of a sentence only.

ii. in the middle of a two-clause sentence only.

iii. in either position.

b. Use your comparison table to write a paragraph comparing log tables with calculators. Write one or two sentences for each line of your chart. Use the words you studied in (a) on pages 43 and 44

Part 1

1. **Listening** — 'Information processing'

   a. A living brain can be thought of as a device for processing information. Information reaches the brain through, for example, the eye. Name other ways in which input about the world reaches the brain. What is the output of a brain?

   b. A computer is a man-made device for processing information. There are several ways in which different computers are able to obtain input, and several ways in which output can be produced. You're going to listen to a short talk about these input and output devices now. Before you start to listen, copy the diagram into your notebook, leaving space to write where you see ....

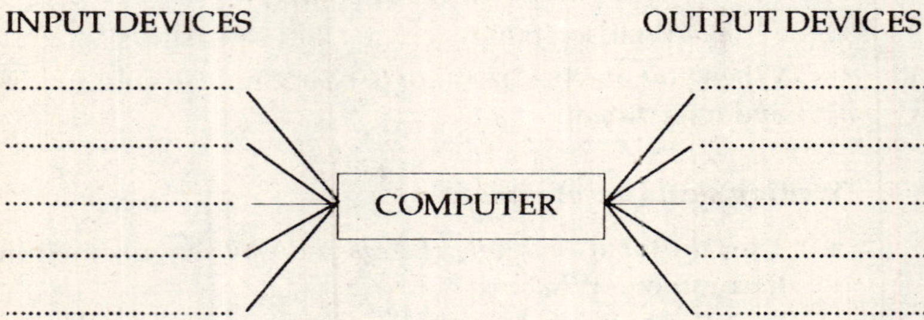

   Now check your answers carefully (including your spelling!).

2. **Language focus** — 'Computer hardware'

   a. *Using intelligent guesswork, complete these definitions of some of the items you have just listed, writing them in your notebook.*

      i. A .... is an output device which prints lines of output onto paper.

      ii. A .... is an output device which can draw graphs, pictures and charts.

iii. A .... is an input device on which you can draw. using a special pen.

iv. A .... is an .... device containing a cathode-ray tube, like a TV screen.

v. A card-reader is .... punched cards.

vi. A paper-tape punch .... punched tape.

vii. A sound synthesiser .... sounds which make words.

b. Look back for names of devices which end in *-er*. Make a list of them, and write down the associated verb (e.g. a computer — compute). Notice, though, a *punch*.

3. **Writing** — 'Are computers better than human brains?'

Using the chart below, write a paragraph comparing a human brain with a computer. Use all the information in the chart, but don't just copy the words : be more original ! Use the words *however* , *while*, *whereas* to make your comparisons clearer.

	HUMAN BRAIN	COMPUTER
WEIGHT	about 1.5 kg	from a few grams to tonnes
ENERGY SOURCE	blood glucose	electricity
TEMPERATURE NEEDED	fairly steady	not very sensitive to change
NO. OF PARTS	approx 10^{11}	approx 10^{11} (100000000,000)
LOCATION OF PARTS	inside skull	could even be in different countries
MEMORY	probably unlimited capacity	capacity limited by technology
SPEED OF CALCULATION	quite slow	extremely fast

4. **Reading** — 'Computer threatens marriage broker

a. *Skim the text below to obtain the gist.*

Computer threatens marriage broker

Clad in white sarong and black coat, with an umbrella tucked under his arm, a once-familiar figure in Sri Lankan households with marriageable sons and daughters is slowly being persuaded aside by modern technology.

Computer dating, introduced to Sri Lanka a little more than a year ago, is becoming a serious threat to the *Magal Kapuwa* — the traditional marriage broker.

For hundreds of years the match-maker has been a respected figure in this island nation where culture and religion encourage social conservatism ! Now he faces the challenge of hi-tech systems which are winning over customers by the day.

"Up to 7,000 names of people seeking partners are already in our computer bank and we get up to 30 callers every day," said Cynthia Dissanayake, manager of an agency in Colombo.

The firm *Jayamangale* (Sinhalese for "wedding bells") assures applicants it will refund their money if they do not find a suitable partner within six months. Tradition, however, still holds in some aspects of marriage in this predominantly Buddhist society, which also has large Hindu, Moslem and Christian communities.

"More than 95 per cent of applicants specify that their marriage partner should come from the same caste, said Dissanayake, whose own marriage was arranged neither by broker nor computer.

Clutching a sheaf of horoscopes, the traditional marriage broker would trudge from house to house usually in his home town area, looking for potential brides and grooms for his customers. At his fingertips were details of the class and caste of his clients, their financial standing and particulars of their family trees — all vital elements in the Sri Lankan social system.

Broker's services were mostly solicited by parents anxious that a son or daughter should marry the "correct" person and not fall victim to the wiles of love, which even in modern-day Sri Lanka is frowned upon. Match-making through a broker also helped ensure that girls' parents did not fall for the ploys of smooth operators seeking the dowry of cash and property given by wealthy fathers to their daughters.

Built up over centuries, the traditional relationship between brokers and conservative families continues today — although not as strongly as a few decades ago. The first threat to the marriage broker came from the advertising pages of national newspapers. Today, column after column of "brides wanted" and "grooms wanted" ads fill the Sunday papers.

Many marriage brokers survived this phenomenon, but they acknowledge they face a bigger threat from computer-dating agencies which for a fee of around $ 15 provide clients with a list of five or six potential partners. The process takes just a day or two, but "instant" lists can be provided for foreigners visiting the country — and such applicants are on the increase, Dissanayake said. Horoscopes remain a vital ingredient in match-making, with up to 90 per cent of applicants requesting this extra "insurance .

Most applicants are Sinhalese Buddhists, who prefer partners of the same religion. Moslems and Hindu Tamils prefer the age-old tradition of making a match through family arrangements and very few seek computer assistance.

Sometimes applicants have romantic notions that even computer technology cannot match — such as to be paired with a movie star.

In the hope of improving their lives, many applicants look for a partner who is better educated, fluent in English and above them in social standing, Dissanayake said. Computer-dating firms do not make a point of following up matches, so they have no accurate assessment of their success rate — although Dissanayake said clients only occasionally" asked for their money back after six months.

It may be sometime, however, before the traditional match-maker is forced completely out of business. According to recent statistics, Sri Lanka's 16 million population includes 4.7 million of 'marriageable' age between 15 and 29. —Compass News Features.

T.B. Peramunetilleke
(from *The Hindu*)

b. Now look back at the text and note the kinds of information (name, etc) needed by a match-maker. Invent two or three main headings under which all this information can be classified. What other information will be needed?

c. Discuss whether you would prefer your own marriage to be arranged by a traditional marriage broker, through the national newspapers, or by a computer. Give your reasons.

Part 2

1. **Reading** — 'A typical computer'

The diagram below shows the main parts of a computer. Can you guess the name or function of any of these parts? After making some guesses, copy the diagram into your notebook and add the correct labels, which you'll find as you read the text.

All computers, large or small, have essentially the same main parts, and they all require connection to a power source, often mains electricity. Perhaps the most important part of any computer is its control centre, or central processing unit (CPU). The CPU receives input, sends work to other parts of the computer, and then collects results and sends them to the output devices. Closely connected with the CPU is the arithmetic unit, which is where the computer calculates, sorts and compares bits of data. The memory is where instructions, data and results are stored until they are needed. A computer has two kinds of main memory. It has a built-in memory, which contains a permanent store of operating instructions. This is known as ROM – read only memory – since these instructions cannot be altered, but can only be read. The other kind of main memory is RAM (random access memory), a short-term memory, which stores input and results until they are needed. When the power supply is disconnected, anything held in RAM is erased. Because built-in memories are not very large, most computers have a backing store in which information is stored on paper tape or cards, magnetic tape or magnetic disc. A recent development in this field is a laser disc. When information in the backing store is needed, the cards, tapes or discs are loaded using the appropriate input device. Finally, computers have a clock which controls the synchronisation of all operations. Input and output devices, though not strictly part of the computer itself, are clearly essential. Computers still need their human operators!

2. **Language focus** — 'Types of computers and their uses'

There are some mistakes in the English in this next passage. Find them and correct them.

The first computer to be developed were all large mainframe computers, and these type of computer is still very much today used. A modern mainframe is can carry out many different job at same time and can be use simultaneous with many users. Each user accesses the mainframe through a terminal who acts as input device and output device both. The store backing for a mainframe is keeped on magnetic tapes which are kept in data storage cabinets. A very large storing back known as a databank. Nowadays, mainframes are in common use by large organisations such as airlines, railways and hotel chains for to centralise their bookings and reservations. Any number of terminals can to be situate anywhere in the world.

Minicomputers are cheapest, smallest and slowest than mainframes. They rarely occupy more than one room, and often used for a particular kind of work, such as data analysis in a research laboratory. Microcomputer are cheaper and smaller and slower than. Although they are less powerful, but they are more flexible since they are portable. and compact. They often known as PCs (personal computers) since there are enough cheap for some individuals to buy. Micros are even found in some primary school in countries such as India, the USSR and the UK which are trying to encourage new generation of computer-literate children.

3. **Role play** — 'Explaining about computers'

Work in pairs.

Student A : You are a schoolmaster, and you have heard that next year your school will be given a microcomputer. You are not at all sure what that is, or what the school will use it for. Prepare a list of questions to ask your son, who is on holiday from his studies at university.

Student B : You are an engineering student visiting your schoolmaster father. You expect he will ask you to tell him about computers. Prepare what you can tell him.

Start when you are both ready.

Writing — 'Microcomputers'

Write a letter to your son at university asking him to explain the potential uses of the microcomputer your school will be given.
(or)
Write a letter to your schoolmaster father explaining the micro-computer and its possible uses in his school.

Follow-up

1. **Comprehension check**

Look back at the text on page 53 and say whether these statements are true or false. Correct the false ones.

a. Computers always require mains electricity.
b. The CPU controls the other parts of the computer.
c. The results of all calculations are kept in the backing store.
d. ROM can be destroyed by disconnecting the energy source.
e. RAM is not a permanent memory.
f. The timing of operations in all parts of the computer is controlled from the same place.
g. A backing store can be of any size.
h. Human operators 'communicate' with computers using the input and output devices.

2. **Language check**

Your teacher will dictate a short passage to you from this week's lessons. Write down what is said, then look back and check.

3. Language development

Look back at the texts in Parts 1 and 2 (pages 46-53) and list all the verbs which tell you things computers can do, such as sort and compare. You should find at least ten more, if you include things input and output devices can do.

For each of these verbs, find a noun. Use a dictionary if you want to.

For example,

SORT – sorting

COMPARE – comparison

Your teacher will help you to check.

4. Writing skills development

You have been asked to write a short and simple explanation of what a computer is for a children's book. Write about sixty words, and draw a simple diagram to help them understand. Write in the present tense, and make your sentences short — but correct!

Computers Unit 2

New frontiers

Preparation

NEW FRONTIERS

1. Language development

a. First, make sure you can pronounce all the words in column A correctly. Then try to match each word in column A with its meaning in column B. Work with your neighbour.

A	B
fiction	not belonging to the earth
fantasy	electronic device producing awareness of the surroundings
extraterrestrial	device composed of silicon
robot	not factual
sensor	material whose conductivity at room temperature lies between that of metals and insulators
natural language	wild imagination
artificial intelligence	the faculty of verbal expression and the use of words in human communication
chip	machine which can perform some of the actions of a human being or animal
semi-conductor	electronic device which can perform a range of basic logical functions upon given signals
microprocessor	the capacity of a computer for learning and decision taking similar to human intelligence

b. You have just looked at the words 'microprocessor' and 'semi -conductor'. The prefix 'micro-' means 'small' and the prefix 'semi-' means 'half'. Think of six other words, three with the prefix 'micro-' and three with the prefix 'semi-'. Use them in sentences of your own . Compare your work with your neighbour's.

2. Oral practice

Classification is the systematic arrangement of persons or things in groups or under specific headings, based on features, characteristics, etc. For example, stone', 'water' and 'oxygen' can be classified under the headings 'solid , 'liquid' and 'gas', respectively. 'Iron' and 'wood' can be classified under the headings 'metallic substances' and 'non-metallic substances'. Similarly, animals can be classified into 'domestic' and 'wild' categories.

Now try to classify computers under different headings. State the basis of the classification. Work in consultation with your neighbour. If you have any difficulty, your teacher will help you.

3. Language development

Here is a list of useful expressions. Make sure you know what each one means.

orientation towards
in view of
call for
on the part of
on the lines of
resort to

Now fill in the gaps in the passage below using these expressions.

Computer education in universities and colleges today leaves much to be desired. .... the importance of the subject., much thought needs to be given to the improvement of computer education at these levels. It is of little use teaching computing .... the traditional, theoretical approach to the subject. On the contrary, it .... a great deal of imagination .... the computer lecturer to present his subject in a clear and interesting way. Rather than theorise about computing principles, he must .... actual demonstrations and hands-on experience in the classroom. The really valuable part of computer learning is an .... the quick solution of everyday problems.

4. Oral practice

Work in groups of two or three.

a. What are some of the areas of activity in which computers are being used today?

b. Are you aware of some specific uses to which computers are put?

c. What possibilities do you think there are for the development of computers in the future?

Part 1

NEW FRONTIERS

1. **Reading** — 'Science fiction'

a. *Note down your answers to these questions.*

   i. Name some writers of science fiction.

   ii. What are some of the themes in science fiction?

   iii. Do you think that science fiction could have any harmful effects on society?

   iv. Does science fiction sometimes come true?

b. Skim the text on science fiction below and locate

   i. a paragraph which states the major themes of science fiction.

   ii. a paragraph which defines and describes science fiction.

   iii. a paragraph listing the features of science fiction.

   iv. a paragraph which raises doubts about the effects of science fiction.

   v. a paragraph relating the history of science fiction.

Try to do this in less than two minutes.

A. Science fiction is one of the most popular forms of literature. It commands a very wide reading public. Many writers all over the world are trying to produce it. As the name itself indicates, it is a mixture of fiction and reality where adventures are set against the background of tomorrow. It is this orientation towards the future which endears it to young people and those in the forefront of science. Some of the greatest writers of science fiction such as Arthur Clarke, Isaac Asimov, Robert Heinlein, John Taine, Edward Smith, Leo Szilard, Otto Frisch, Fred Hoyle, Chad Oliver, Stanislaw Lem and Norbert Wiener were themselves renowned scientists or engineers.

B. Science fiction is as old as human fantasy. Plato, Cyrano le Bergerac, Voltaire, Edgar Allan Poe, Jules Verne and H G Wells made their contribution to it long before it became a separate literary form. The name itself was invented only in 1926 by Hugo Gernsback, an American, who founded in 1928 the magazine *Amazing Stories*. Science fiction entered a new epoch in 1937, when John W Campwell Jr took over the editorship of *Astounding Science Fiction*. It now began to assume a story pattern. Not only did it include the element of scientific speculation, as it had done till now, but concerned itself with those of character and human drama as well. Since then the volume of science fiction produced has been on the increase. Even general magazines, radio, television and feature films have begun to make use of it.

C. Some of the major themes dealt with by science fiction are space travel to and from other planets, solar systems and galaxies; exploration, settlement and exploitation of other worlds; encounters with or between extraterrestrial life forms; time travel to the future or the past; psychological and biological changes in man brought about by nature or science and similar changes in other species; supernatural powers and talents, achieved either through technology or the advancement of such 'fringe sciences' as parapsychology; and science, applied directly or indirectly, to human relations for either constructive or destructive purposes.

D. Some of the features of science fiction are as follows. It is highly entertaining, as there is always plenty of dynamic action, breath-taking adventure and strong emotions in it. At the same time, it may be said to be the most instructive of all the literary genres. It arouses the curiosity of the people to know things and enables them to learn many things that they could not have known. It fires the imagination of its readers and lures them into a flight of fantasy into realms unknown. The impossible does not exist in its pages. It is amazing to note how science fiction has been capable of predicting the shape of events to come. Unlike the other forms of literature that are tied down to this world of ours, science fiction is unfettered in its conception and treatment. The novelty and infinite variety are perhaps its greatest advantages. All these features of science fiction give us an idea of what this many-faceted literature is. It is a fine example of the synthesis of science and art.

E. There is, however, one disturbing aspect of science fiction that needs consideration, in view of its tremendous sociological impact. Like any other instrument of knowledge, science fiction has in it the potential for abuse. Whether it will spur people on to extend their terrestrial wars to outer space is a question that only the future can decide. The present situation calls for a noble humanist attitude and a high moral responsibility on the part of the science fiction writer.

c. Look back at the passage and try to guess the meanings of the underlined words from the context or their form. If you cannot, ask your neighbour. Your teacher will explain the words later.

d. Look back at your answers to (a) on page 58 and read the relevant paragraph of the text carefully to compare your views with those of the author.

Discuss with a partner what you have learnt by reading this passage, and whether you had thought of something the author does not mention.

> **Learner awareness**
> You can improve your own English considerably by reading widely. It is best to read something you enjoy, so if you like science fiction, you can improve your English and enjoy yourself at the same time.

2. **Language focus — 'Robots'**

Robots were once only fictional. Now, computerisation has made them a reality. Some of the words in the box belong in the text below. Read the text carefully once, then try to fill in the gaps with the most appropriate word.

person	sequence	commonly	sensors
benevolent	efficiency	version	limited
mechanical	malevolent	past	future
react	gripping	artificial	numerous
sense	correspond	refer	machine

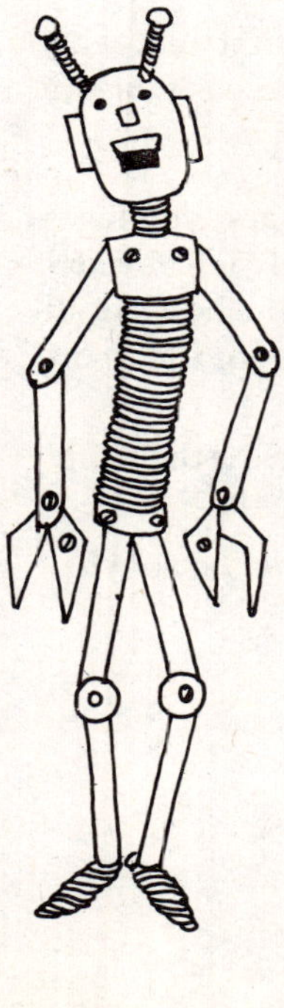

Robots

A robot is a .... which can perform some of the actions of a human being or animal. The kind of robot that is now .... in use is a machine which carries out a .... of operations under computer control. The association of robots with science fiction has served to project them as nightmarish, ... automatons. But the industrial robots now in use seem anything but dreadful. They are the .... arms of support. They can tirelessly perform monotonous and exhausting physical tasks with maximum .... and minimum supervision.

A newer .... of robots is the one with electronic 'senses'. The robot is fitted with .... in the form of radar devices and microphones with which it could detect movements and hear noises. The robot's radar and microphones .... to human eyes and ears. In addition to 'sight' and 'hearing' the robot can have a .... of 'touch', too, via pressure pads which show how tightly they are .... something, and can also sense heat and cold. Though human beings can .... in a great number of ways to the information supplied to the brain through the senses, a robot's responses are ....

Robots of the .... might be endowed with .... intelligence. They would then perform not merely mechanical operations, but react to unforeseen circumstances and make decisions. They might play games, solve problems and use natural language.

Check your answer with your neighbour's.

3. **Writing** — 'Robots'

Do task (a) or (b) — (a) is easier.

a. Write a paragraph about robots. In your first sentence, define a robot. Then, classify robots on the basis of the information given in the text.

b. It is some time in the not-too-distant future, and you have decided to order a household robot, which will be designed to suit your requirements. First, list the household tasks which you expect the robot to perform, then sort these tasks into broad categories.
Write a paragraph (which is part of a letter) to the robot factory stating what you require. Begin like this:

There are several types of task my robot must be able to perform. Firstly, ...

NEW FRONTIERS

Part 2

1. **Reading — 'Computers of the future'**

   a. Write down brief answers to the following.

      i. How do computers of today differ from those of the past

      ii. What are some of the tasks that computers are likely to execute in the future?

      iii. Do you think that it will be possible for computers to behave like human beings?

      iv. What are some of the objections that are likely to be raised against the use of computers?

   b. Now study-read the passage. Follow this procedure:

      i. Skim for gist , and write one (or more) of the words past, present, or future next to each paragraph.

      ii. Compare your answers to (a) with the passage.

      iii. Make brief notes using the following framework:

   A. Computers in the past were: i.
   ii.
   iii.
   iv.
   v.

   B. Computers at present are: i.
   ii.
   iii.
   iv.
   v.

   C. Computers in future will be: i.
   ii.
   iii.
   iv.
   v.

D. The possible grounds of objection against computers is

i.

ii.

iii.

iv.

v.

Check your notes with a neighbour.

Computers of the future

i. Over the last fory years computers have developed dramatically. They have become smaller and cheaper, and more and more powerful. The first computers could do relatively few calculations a second, whereas the present mainframe can carry out millions of instructions each second. In the past only highly trained computer experts were able to use computers. But, as they became cheaper and smaller and easier to operate, many people such as doctors, teachers, librarians, architects, artists and even persons at home are now finding that a computer can help them. These trends will, probably, continue in the future, too.

ii The possible development of computers in the future might be on these lines. The time may come when owning a computer will be as common as owning a wrist watch. In future houses may be erected with built-in computers controlling everything from paying bills to opening doors and regulating the entry of people. Computers functioning on the basis of sensors of different kinds and executing a wide variety of tasks will be a common feature of the times to come. For example, they may control all lights in the house by switching them on and off as people enter or get out of the rooms. They may control heating, air-conditioning, opening windows, etc with the help of electronic signals. Automatic plant watering systems based on humidity sensors and machines taking messages and replying in human voices using speech synthesisers are among the amazing possibilities in the future.

iii . But the main thrust of the development of computers in the future is likely to be in the form of efforts to make them reflect the human capacity to reason. Research is on to find ways of investing computers with artificial intelligence. Computers in future would behave intelligently, react to situations and take decisions. They may solve problems the way human experts do, resorting to commonsense thinking. Future systems will have a subtle command of natural language in different subjects and provide reliable machine translation between various natural languages. That the new research might make it possible for us to have a chat with the expert system is a hope for the future.

The prospect for this future, however, may still be bleak for a long time to come in the under-developed and developing countries of the world. Apart from the fact that not all can afford these intelligent machines of the future, the big question that arises is this: Do we really want such machines? Even with the existing machines there is a lot of concern about the amount of personal information about people held in data banks. Such information in wrong hands could easily be used to discriminate against people. There is also the possibility of interception of computer messages and alteration of the information passed. The fears of unemployment resulting from the use of computers may prove, in the long run, to be unwarranted. Not only will the computers still need skilled workers to programme and control them, but many jobs will be available in the fields of education, welfare and health care, entertainment, sport and craft. But what must be worrying the minds of people is the possible dehumanising influence of computer technology. There will always be the nagging threat of artificial intelligence denying us our individuality and freedom. Machines may become super-intelligent, overtake human beings and rule the earth.

2. **Listening**—'Silicon Valley and Apple'

a. You are going to listen to a talk about Silicon Valley and Apple. In pairs quickly discuss what you know about Silicon Valley and Apple.

b. Listen carefully and take notes. If you need help, a chart like this may help you organise your notes:

SILICON VALLEY		APPLE	
where located		what it is	
why called so		who is its co-founder and chairman	
what it was 50 years ago		his background	
what it is now		his contribution	
its economic status		its economic status	
how it can be described		its impact	

3. **Discussion** — 'Artificial intelligence'

a. *Read the short article on page 67 and note down the types of human-like behaviour some computer systems are now capable of.*

Artificial intelligence based systems get into US industry

Computer systems endowed with 'artificial intelligence' have begun to make their mark on American manufacturing. Computer vision systems, some of which can 'see' the difference between a bad and good circuit board on an assembly line, made up nearly a quarter of the $ 1 billion artificial intelligence (AI) industry in 1986.

'Natural language' systems are also rapidly coming of age, with some $ 60 millions spent in 1986 for products that respond to naturally spoken or written English. One industry analyst predicts that 1988 will bring a typewriter that prints whatever is spoken to it. But knowledge-based 'expert systems' are pressing researchers even further towards an understanding of how human beings think.

Already, software programmes are being written that attempt to utilise the 'rules of thumb' that human experts follow when solving problems. Such programmes mimic the logic of human specialists, from mechanics to accountants. Some systems are crammed with knowledge acquired from dozens of human professionals. Codified inside a computer programme, their cumulative expertise can be applied *en masse,* and at lightning speed, to previously insolvable manufacturing puzzles.

Within the last two years there have been practical applications for AI technology emerging in nearly every industry, say AI specialists. At Boeing, one of the world's largest builders of commercial aircraft, expert systems development is a priority. Using a system that generates manufacturing plans directly from three-dimensional computer-aided designs, Boeing can determine the manufacturing schedule for certain parts, or a class of parts.
— USIS

b. **If the trend towards AI continues, how will it affect human beings? If you can, classify the effects under some general headings, such as 'employment'.**

Be ready to report back when your teacher asks you to.

NEW FRONTIERS

Follow-up

1. Oral practice

Look back at the notes you took on page 66 *. Work in pairs. Take it in turns to ask and answer questions about Silicon Valley and Apple.*

2. Comprehension check

Look back at the text on pages 64 - 65 *and say what these expressions refer to :*

a. *(line 11)* These trends .... (what trends?)
b. *(line 21)* For example .... (example of what?)
c. *(line 43)* this future .... (what future?)
d. *(line48)* such machines .... (what kind of machines?)

3. Language check

Look at the following sentences and punctuate them. Check by looking back at lines 6-11 of the text on page 109.

> in the past only highly trained computer experts were able to use computers but as they became cheaper and smaller and easier to operate many people such as doctors teachers librarians architects artists and even persons at home are now finding that a computer can help them

4. Language development

Look back at the text 'Computers of the future' and notice how the following modal verbs are used:

can could will would may might

Classify them according to the degree of probability they express:

definite (100% probability)
probable
possible
impossible (0% probability)

5. Oral practice

Look at these headlines

Computers Replace Child's Real Parents

Computers to Replace Marriage Brokers

Meteorologists Redundant Computers Take Over

Computers Declare Strike

Computer Awarded Ph.D

Perfect Spelling by Computer

Computer Diagnosis More Accurate Than Doctor's!

Using the modal verbs you studied in the last excercise, make statements expressing how probable you think these events are. For example :

A computer will never replace a child's real parents.

NEW FRONTIERS

Computers Unit 3

Preparation

1. Oral practice

In pairs, discuss the following :

a. How would the introduction of the computer affect the employment situation in India?

b. Do you know any examples of computerisation in India?

c. What do you think of the inclusion of computers as a subject of study in the schools in India?

2. Language development

Work in pairs. Try to guess the meaning of the underlined word in each of these sentences. The context will help you.

a. Some people argue that computerisation will aggravate the unemployment problem.

b. One of India's priorities is to grow more food.

c. There are countless opportunities for work for qualified computer personnel.

d. The crux of the matter is training. Without adequate training Indian industry cannot progress.

e. Many projects are being held up because of a paucity of funds.

f. The Indian government is taking steps to streamline the working of the railways through computerisation.

g. Indian agriculture is affected by the vagaries of the weather, so even computers cannot produce accurate production forecasts.

h. To deepen our understanding, it helps us to look at problems from different perspectives.

Learner awareness
When you come across a word whose meaning you do not know, the context will often help you to guess the approximate meaning.

3. Reading skills development

a. Before reading the following text, make a list of things which you feel may have been made possible by the introduction of computers in Indian Airlines.

b. As you read the text, go through your list. Place a tick (✓) by the items you had thought of, and add to your list any things mentioned in the text which you had not thought of.

Today seat reservation in IA can be done instantly with the aid of a computer at the four international airports as well as a dozen domestic stations. The remaining stations in the country are connected to the central system by teletype links. Tickets are printed automatically in the major cities.

Another facility that has been made possible by computerisation is the Flight Information System which provides updated information on the departure and arrival times of flights. This information can be displayed on screens in the passenger lounges.

Meteorological information is of vital importance to a flight; the crew will find such information most useful, since flights may have to be delayed or cancelled or diverted if the weather does not permit safe landing or take-off. The computer provides up-to-the-minute information on the conditions in the airports, and the information can be displayed on the screen at any airport from where a plane is to take off.

c. Did your list help you to read more efficiently?

4. Writing skills development

Write definitions by making sentences using one expression from each of the three columns, and adding the necessary grammar.

The arithmetic unit	chart	which can perform some of the movements of a person or animal
A computer	device	which shows the sequence of steps in a programme for solving a problem on a computer
A flowchart	machine	which tells the computer what to do
A microprocessor	part of the computer	which can accept and process data and output the result
A printer	set of instructions	in which calculations are done
A program	silicon chip	which can print out information from a computer
A robot		which can do the same jobs as the parts inside a computer

COMPUTERS IN INDIA

Part 1

1. **Language focus — 'An adjective inventing task'**

Look at the following expressions:

voltage-controlled oscillator
time-consuming process
ferrous-oxide-coated tape

Notice how the past participle (-*ed*) and present participle (-*ing*) forms of verbs are used to form compound adjectives.

i. The first of these expressions means '(an oscillator) which is controlled by voltage'
What do the other two mean ?

ii. What is the difference between

computer–controlled machine

and computer–controlling machine

iii. Now make similar, meaningful expressions by choosing one item from each column. How many expressions can you make?

binary	-aided	circuits
card	-coded	decimal
computer	-coupled	design
data	-loading	logic
emitter	-made	machine
ready	-processing	packages
self	-punching	systems

iv. Can you think of any more examples from computer science?

2. **Reading** — 'Employing computers'

a. *Discuss the following in small groups.*

i. Do you think that the introduction of computers will lead to unemployment ?

ii. Are there any advantages in the computerisation of work in large establishments ? If so, what are they ?

iii. Do you know of any Indian organisations which have introduced computerisation? In which area would computerisation be useful ?

b. Skim the text below and

i. say whether the text is
argumentative
narrative
imaginative

ii. Choose the best alternative to complete this statement:
The aim of the author is...

1. to compare the computer revolution with the Industrial Revolution.

2. to suggest a solution to the problem of unemployment.
3. to describe the benefits of computerisation.

iii. Now read the text more carefully and answer the questions which follow it.

Employing Computers

The most vehement opposition to computerisation comes from people who believe that it will lead to unemployment. Their basic argument is that computers will aggravate the present situation of unemployment by snatching away jobs from human beings. By linking unemployment with computerisation, they have created a seemingly valid issue to serve their vested interests perfectly. Is the cause of unemployment a matter of too few jobs for too many people? A closer look suggests that it is not so. Consider our priorities. We have to

— grow more food
— produce more cloth
— build more houses, roads, bridges
— provide better education.

In fact, there is so much to be done that this list can be extended endlessly. Why is there so much unemployment if there is so much to be done? On the one hand we have people who are without work, and on the other we have countless jobs which are not being done. What is the reason for this paradox? The crux of the matter is that we do not have enough funds at our disposal. If we had adequate funds, everybody could find work. Thus the cause of unemployment is not a lack of jobs but a paucity of funds.

Indian Railways have been able to save as much as Rs 27 crores last year by computerising their wagon transport system. In the past this system was notorious for delay and inefficiency. Computers successfully removed bottlenecks by streamlining procedures. Thus they generated savings of a very high magnitude.

In India the vagaries of the weather play havoc with agriculture. Every year crores of rupees are lost by drought or flood. If we could feed into the computer the data about rainfall in each region for the last 20 years and, by analysis, identify the areas prone to drought or to flood, then we can take corrective action before calamity strikes.

Thus it can be asserted confidently that computerisation is a valid and relevant medium for:

— increasing productivity and efficiency;
— bringing about savings in cost;
— generating funds and consequently creating additional employment;
— bringing about greater all-round progress to the country.

A very close parallel exists between the present computer revolution and the Industrial Revolution of the nineteenth century. During the Industrial Revolution there was a similar hue and cry against mechanisation. People argued that machines would take away jobs from men and cause unemployment. Looking back, we can now get a different perspective of what really happened. The Industrial Revolution did not cause unemployment. Today more people are employed on machines than were employed before industrialisation when there were no machines. Automation resulted in efficiency and a reduction of cost leading to generation of more funds. These funds are reinvested to generate more economic activity and consequently create more employment for people. By linking computerisation with unemployment, trade union leaders are doing the country a great disservice. Let us take a lesson from history.

(Source : Sanjay Kankaria in *Computers Today*, November 1986).

c. Explain what the following items refer to:

their (line 3)
we (line 12)
this system (line 30)
they (line 34)

d. What is a paradox? Explain the paradox mentioned in paragraph 2. Can you give an example of a paradox from your own knowledge or experience?

e. How many examples of the use of the computer does the author give? What are they?

f. At the end of the first paragraph the author mentions four things that have to be done. Later in the text, the author discusses only one of these. In which lines do you find this ?

g. *Look at the words underlined in the text. Match each word with one of the meanings given below:*

i. smallness of number or quantity; scarcity
ii. view
iii. make worse; make more serious
iv. widely known, especially for something bad
v. the most difficult part of a problem
vi. making more efficient
vii. numerous, a very large number of
viii. loud protest, or expression of alarm or opposition
ix. things to be done first
x. unreasonable or unpredictable acts

3. 3. Language focus — 'Abbreviations'

a. Abbreviations are shortened forms of words. Using abbreviations speeds up one's writing, and is very useful for note-taking in lectures.
Here are some commonly used abbreviations:

bet.	between	↗	increase
orgn.	organisation	↘	decrease
sym	symbol	→	leads to, causes

req.	require	Δlar	triangular
govt.	government	$\therefore$	therefore
adv.	advantage	$\equiv$	equivalent to
eq.	equation	etc.	and so on (et cetera)

Note : There are no 'fixed rules' for abbreviations. Invent your own, but be sure you can still interpret them after some time has elapsed.
Acronyms can also be useful. Some standard ones are:
VDU ROM RAM CPU PC AI BASIC

b. To practise using abbreviations, look back at paragraph 6 of the text on page 76 and make notes.

Compare your notes with your neighbour's. Can you learn anything from each other ?

4. **Listening** — 'The electronics industry in Tamil Nadu'

Listen carefully to the talk on *The electronics industry in Tamil Nadu*.

Note down each of the seven factors which have affected the electronics industry in Tamil Nadu, and for each of these, note down the nature of the problem. The first factor you will hear mentioned is *Finance*. Can you make use of abbreviations ?

Part 2

1. **Language focus** — 'The virus threat'

Read both the following articles quite quickly, and decide which is the livelier, which is more serious, and which is more difficult to understand.

Computer virus hits Delhi varsity

After the recent scare in the US, it is the Delhi University's turn. Computers at the university have been ' hit' by a virus. ASHAR, which gobbles up valuable space in the floppy disks, destroys stored files and sends wrong messages. Its origins are still a matter of speculation.

The virus was discovered around ten days ago when students at the recently-created Centre of Science Education reported having sighted ASHAR almost simultaneously, said Dr Amitava Mukherjee of the University's Department of Physics and Astrophysics.

Dr Mukherjee told *The Hindu* here today that the virus shows itself on the screen when the user operates the directory to recall stored matter. The words 'COPYRIGHT ASHAR' have been frequently noticed. A computer virus represents a programme that is alien to the host system, is free of the intention of the operator and makes copies of itself (like any other biological virus) within the system.

Confirming the presence of ASHAR, a student of the University's Department of Computer Science said the virus had caused a number of disks to be 'reformated'. It could cause 'grave damage' once it acquires the potential to 'infect' the hard disk and other core areas of the computer. The implications of ASHAR are still being assessed, he said.

Dr Mukherjee says the virus is as yet benign and timely steps have ensured that it does not eat into vital programmed matter. The vigilance of an alert student led to counter measures. The possibility of different departments at the University, including the central computer centre, being affected as a result of software being ferried from one place to another is not ruled out. According to a professor at the Computer Science Department, the virus, known to affect a particular software system (called DOSS), has been spread due to widespread use of 'pirated software'.

Consequently, the Department of Physics and Astrophysics has issued its own do's and don'ts. Students and teachers are being told not to borrow unauthorised software, switch off their PCs before starting work (to destroy the virus lodged in the memory), using the directory to locate ASHAR and sticking to a clean disk.

(Source : *The Hindu*, March 1989)

Much Ado About Nothing

The media is known to exaggerate. At times. And even if it does not exaggerate, there is no denying the fact that our media does make and break commodities. And people.

Much as we would like to avoid getting influenced, journalists (this writer included) do lap up news which sells. We may not try to be sensational, but deep down our subconcious our nose

for news sniffs only what smells well.

So when recently, we found news items on Doordarshan and periodicals talking about a virus invading computers, journalists went berserk. Doom in the world outside rings music in a media man's ears, goes an old dictum. That's precisely what occurred.

A respected business fortnightly, not known to resorting to sensationalism to sell copies, carried the virus syndrome as its cover story. Newspapers highlighted the virus report by 'boxing' it.

Within days, the message was sent home: Computers too can suffer from an AIDS-like disease. There was panic in the air. But suprisingly students of computer science as well as professionals and end-users seem undeterred by the scare. Or, at least, those who have not yet been affected by the virus consider the environment quite hunky-dory.

Then why this hue and cry about computer viruses, and how they are creating havoc in the West ? Is it true that there is something called a virus ? Or is it yet another hype in the media ?

The answer is yes.

Yes, computer viruses do exist. Yes, because the entire episode has been blown up by the media. The doom-news syndrome, perhaps, to quote that oft-repeated Shakespearean line, is much ado about nothing.

Source : *Indian Express*, April 1989

b. In groups, study both articles to see how the effect is achieved. Use a chart like this one to help you classify your observations.

	TEXT A	TEXT B
1. CONTENT		
a. Are there many facts (definitions, events, etc)?		
b. Are there many opinions?		
c. Whose opinions are given?		

	TEXT A	TEXT B
2. LANGUAGE		
a. personal (you/we/our etc) or impersonal (passives)?		
b. words used unemotional (e.g. 'virus shows itself') or emotional and exaggerated (e.g. 'virus invading computers')?		

c. When you have to produce written work for other subjects, what effects do you wish to create ? How should you express your meaning? Discuss this with a neighbour.

Learner awareness
Whatever profession you choose to follow, you will have to produce written English in your work. To create a good impression, your written English should be clearly expessed, free from errors, and appropriate to its audience and purpose. These skills take some time to develop, but you can speed up your progress by paying attention to the written style of things you read. For example, if you find one of your textbooks incomprehensible, this might be because it is not well written. Be critical of your own written work – there will almost always be room for improvement. !

2. **Reading** — "The story of Indian Airlines'

a. Work in pairs. Before you read the text on page 82 list at least ten operations necessary to this organisation, such as 'maintain its planes' or 'set up a rota for the crews'. On each item on your list, decide whether computerisation could be beneficial.

b. Work individually.

   i. Read the first sentence in each paragraph quickly and mark the words which express the probable topic of each paragraph.

   ii. Scanning the text, list the main applications of computerisation mentioned.

c. Work in pairs. Try to classify the items from your list of operations (see (a) above) under the headings in your list of main applications.

   Did you think of any operations which are not covered in this text ? Be prepared to report back to the class when your teacher asks you.

Computerisation in India: the Story of Indian Airlines

More than twenty years ago, Indian Airlines decided to computerise some of their operations. These were, to begin with, financial control and inventory control. Five years later, in 1971, one more IBM 1401 system was acquired. The first one had been a tape-based system, but this one was a disk-based system. Besides the earlier operations, advance reservation of seats for passenger flights was now brought within the scope of computerisation.

With the increase in the number of flights and the volume of traffic, the need for a real time system was felt: this is a system in which data input is processed immediately and the result is available instantly to be used as feedback information. In airlines booking, each booking is processed as soon as it is made, so that a completely up-to-date picture of the position is maintained by the computer at all times. In 1983 a real time system was sanctioned for Indian Airlines. It could deal with ten million passengers. A year later, another Central Processing Unit (CPU) and eight disk drives were added. The system could now meet the needs of 15 million passengers.

Today seat reservation in IA can be done instantly with the aid of a computer at the four international airports as well as a dozen domestic stations. The remaining stations in the country are connected to the central system by teletype links. Tickets are printed automatically in the major cities.

Another facility that has been made possible by computerisation is the Flight Information System which provides updated information on the departure and arrival times of flights. This information can be displayed on screens in the passenger lounges.

Meteorological information is of vital importance to a flight; the crew will find such information most useful, since flights may have to be delayed or cancelled or diverted if the weather doe not permit safe landing or take-off. The computer provides up-to-the-minute information on the conditions in the airports, and the information can be displayed on the screen at any airport from where a plane is to take off.

After computerisation, the management information system in IA has become efficient; the management can now have up-to-the-minute reports on the performance data of the airline. The management will require data on capacity utilisation, passenger and cargo transport, income and expenditure with reference to aircraft as well as to each sector of operation, and crew utilisation, to make policy decisions as well as decisions on normal working of the airline. In the past only batch processing of data on a monthly basis was done; but now data are processed instantly and are available on a day-to-day basis. This is an important feature of the present computerisation, and makes it possible for the management to ensure that the total system is profitable and to optimise resource utilisation.

d. *Now answer these questions.*

i. Look at the words which are underlined. Say what they refer to.

ii. What changes occurred in the computerisation in Indian Airlines in the 1970s and early 1980s?

iii. What is a real time system? Why did a real time system become necessary?

iv. How do passengers receive information about departure and arrival times of flights?

v. How does the computer help in ensuring the safety of airline flights? The passage mentions one way. Can you think of any other way in which a computer can make flights safer?

vi. Explain the following terms in your own words.
capacity utilisation (line 46)
sector of operation (line 48)
crew utilisation (line 48)
batch processing of data (lines 50-51)
to optimise resource utilisation (lines 55-56)

3. Discussion — 'Private computer institutes a roaring business!'

a. Look at these advertisements, and discuss the likely motives of the students who join private institutes.

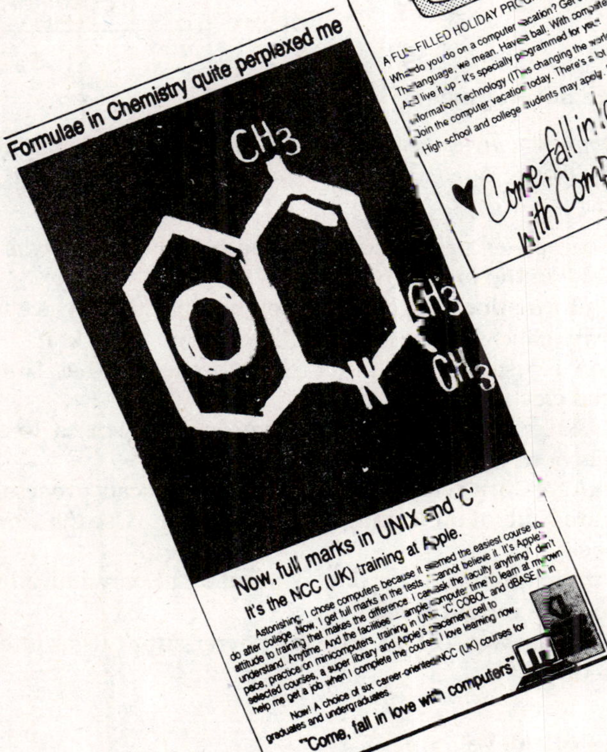

COMPUTERS IN INDIA

4. **Writing** — 'Private computer institutes'

Your cousin wants to take a computer course at a private institute and has asked you for advice. She is thinking of applying to one of the institutes advertised above. Write a letter to her pointing out some comparisons between the institutes, and advising her what to do.

Follow-up

1. **Language development**

Rewrite the following sentences using 'because of', 'on account of', 'owing to', paying careful attention to any necessary changes in grammar.

i. The computer produced nonsense because there was a mistake in the programming.
ii. The information was easily stolen because there were no security checks in the system. (Use the word 'lack'.)
iii. Silicon is used in computer chips because it has some special electrical properties.
iv. The VDU quality was poor because there was a loose connection.
v. Computers are widely used because they can process a vast amount of information at great speed. (Use the word 'capacity'.)
vi. The trade unionists fear that computerisation will lead to large-scale retrenchment.
vii. All the data was lost because the power-supply was interrupted.

2. **Writing skills development**

a. With a partner, look at the notes you took on page 78 Exercise 4. Discuss what recommendations you would make to the Tamil Nadu Government.

With your partner, write a list of recommendations in formal English. Here is an example, which you caan use as a pattern :

1. The software industry should be recognised as an industry by the Government of Tamil Nadu in order to make it eligible for assistance from financial institutions such as ICICI.

3. Language development

Both the present perfect and simple past tenses indicate an action completed in the past. But the present perfect relates it to the present situation. If a definite point of time in the past is indicated, the verb is in the simple past tense and not in the present perfect tense.

Examples : More than twenty years ago Indian Airlines *decided* to computerise some of their operations. (simple past)
By linking unemployment with computerisation they *have created* a valid issue to serve their vested interests perfectly. (present perfect)

Rewrite the following sentences using the present perfect or simple past tense forms of the verbs in brackets.

a. Indian Airlines (introduce) the automatic printing of tickets in major cities.
b. In 1971 Indian Airlines (acquire) one more IBM 1401 system.
c. The number of flights (increase) on important sectors.
d. Last year Indian Airlines (arrange) for provision of data on a day-to-day basis.
e. Indian Airlines (become) very efficient.

4. Oral practice

Student A : You are a reporter, interested in the effects of computerisation in Indian Railways. Prepare to ask questions about efficiency, profitability, safety, freight, passenger services and so on, such as 'Have the railways become more efficient?'

Student B : You are a Publicity Officer with Indian Railways. You want to give a good impression to the reporter, so you will give answers such as 'Efficiency has improved'. Prepare to answer questions, using the present perfect tense.

Start when you are both ready. Pay attention to your grammar.

COMPUTERS IN INDIA

Technology Unit 1

Appropriate technology

Preparation

1. Language development

a. *Match the words in column A with their meanings in column B.*

A	B
i. technology	a. nourishment
ii. appropriate	b. obtaining juices by pressing, crushing, boiling
iii. exploitation	c. dry outer covering of grain, seeds, etc
iv. indigenous	d. unfit to eat
v. innovative	e. thick, sticky, solid mass
vi. porridge	f. applied science
vii. coagulum	g. soft food made by boiling a cereal in water or milk
viii. husk	h. suitable
ix. nutrition	i. utilisation, usually unfairly,for one's own benefit
x. extraction	j. native
xi. inedible	k. having the quality of introducing new things, making changes

b. *Look at the following examples of the use of ' self ' to form words.*

self + reliant	self-reliant
self + sufficient	self-sufficient

Suggest three more expressions beginning with 'self' and write three sentences using them.

c. *Fill in the gaps in the following passage with the prepositions 'to', 'of', 'by', 'between' and 'with'.*

Appropriate technology is a technology that is developed to cater .... the basic needs .... economically poor people. It is not low or primitive technology. Also, it is not concerned .... only the small-scale technology. Appropriate technology lies somewhere .... a traditional and a modern technology. It is particularly easy to operate and can be maintained .... less skilled persons. The special feature .... this technology is that it can be applied .... a variety .... rural needs.

2. Oral practice

Look at this definition.

'Appropriate technology is that technology which is economically feasible within the resources available, which is culturally acceptable and which is environmentally harmless.'

Discuss this with your partner and define the following, trying to use the formal language of the definition you have just read.

a. high technology
b. traditional technology
c. laser technology

3. Writing skills development

Write a paragraph on appropriate technology, developing the hints that are provided below.

a. low capital investment per unit of output

b. small-scale operations

c. use of local materials wherever possible

d. high adaptability to local skills-labour

e. ease of understanding and maintenance by the user without a high level of education

f. unpolluting and benign with reference to the physical environment

g. use of natural and renewable energy sources such as wind, power, solar energy, water power, pedal power and bio-gas.

Part 1

1. **Listening** — 'Different types of technology'

   a. *Working in small groups try to answer these questions.*

      i. What is technology?

      ii. Can you classify the different types of technology? Can you give examples?

      iii. What are the features of the different types of technology?

   b. Listen to a brief talk about technology and take notes on the different types of technology.

2. **Reading** — 'Pedal power'

Read these two paragaraphs of the passage on pedal power. Then arrange the twelve sentences which follow and write the next four paragraphs of the passage.

> The rural and urban poor in India expend their muscle power every day to provide the basic necessities of life. An example is the widespread use of the bicycle. It should be noted that the power produced by a human being cannot match that produced by the internal combustion engine and electric motor. But due to the shortage of fuels and undependable electric supply, innovative use of human energy may have to be considered seriously.

The advent of the internal combustion engine and electric motor ended the use of pedal power in small-scale industries and in agricultural processing. Even though India has abundant human power and over 40 million bicycles are used for transportation, the pedal power potential has not been fully realised in small-scale agricultural activities.

a. The first type is a stationary one, in which bicycle parts like the frame, crank, chain and freewheel are used to produce a rotating motion.

b. The second type of pedal power device is a modified bicycle which can be used both as a vehicle for transportation and a prime mover.

c. This modified bicycle is called a dual-purpose bicycle.

d. There are two types of pedal power devices in existence today.

e. This rotary motion can be used to operate machines such as threshers, winnowers, pumps, woodworking lathes and metal lathes.

f. It is in fact a versatile mechanism which can be used for transportation as well as power production.

g. The dual-purpose bicycle can be used to power small-scale agricultural implements and equipment used in rural industries.

h. The dual-purpose bicycle has a permanent attachment and a modified broad stand cum carrier.

i. These are a few examples :
- paddy thresher
- winnower
- groundnut shell remover
- small water pump
- grinder

j. Thus the technologists who advocate appropriate technology are confident that the exploitation of pedal power for various uses will make the rural poor self-reliant and self-sufficient as far as their energy needs are concerned.

k. It can also be used to power a drill, woodworking lathe, metal lathes and circular saw.

1. The use of the dual-purpose bicycle will also help them to provide employment to the unemployed and unskilled, and decrease their dependence on outside power sources.

If you find it difficult, search for key words and phrases that refer to

a. a pedal power device (first)
b. a pedal power device (second)
c. uses of the dual-purpose bicycle
d. conclusion

and then arrange the sentences.

3. **Reading** — 'Bicycle-operated domestic pump'

a. Skim through the passage and suggest suitable headings for the four paragraphs.

b. Read the passage and answer the questions that follow it. Do not worry about the underlined words. They are for exercise 2b in the Follow-up lesson.

The Centre for Water Resources, College of Engineering, took up an appropriate technology project in 1976 and completed it in 1978. This project is a practical project specially designed to suit the rural conditions in India. Since the villages in India face acute power shortage, it was hoped that this project, when implemented, would prove a boon to the rural masses.

In this project the principles of using stationary pedal power to pump water for domestic and field uses is brought out. The pump used is an ordinary reciprocating type. This device consists of a permanent stand made of G.I. sheet with pipes welded to its bottom which is hammered into the earth close to the pump at a pre-calculated distance. The front wheel of the cycle is kept immovable by keeping it on a stand or some other fixture. Thus the bicycle is held rigid.

To pump water, all that one has to do is to sit on the bicycle seat and pedal. The drive is transmitted from the front sprocket to the rear wheel which now acts as a flywheel and transmits the power through the second chain to the pump. As the pump is a positive displacement one, water is pumped out even at low speeds. Also, no priming is necessary. After the use, the clip is released and the chain is opened. Then the bicycle can be lifted from the permanent stand and used as a normal two-wheeler.

The cost involved is very low when compared to the cost of a conventional motor for domestic use. The pumping test proved to be a success. An average man can easily pedal for 2 hours continuously without much fatigue. This will serve as a good exercise and prove to be a boon for small farmers and domestic users.

i. List the tools and equipment needed to make a bicycle operate a domestic pump.

ii. Look at the following diagram of a pedal-powered pump. Label the parts.

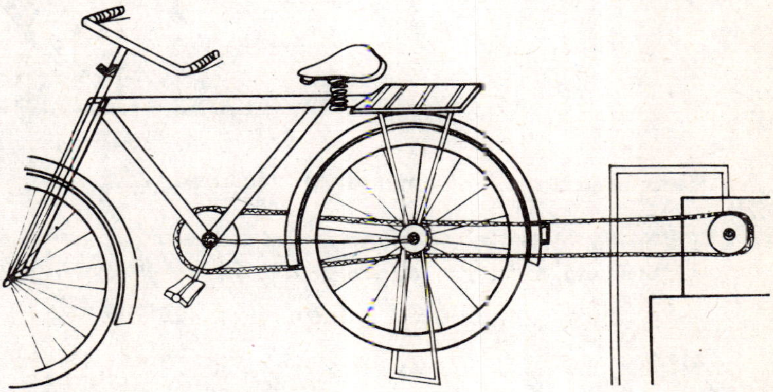

4. **Discussion — 'Pedal power in Indian villages'**

Discuss in pairs how pedal power can help people in Indian villages. Be ready to report your views when the teacher asks you to.

Part 2

1. **Language focus — 'Cement from rice husk'**

Fill in the blanks in the following text with suitable verbs in the passive form. Choose, if necessary, from this list of verbs.

mix produce burn obtain use

Rice husk .... from rice mills. It .... in such a large quantity that its disposal sometimes becomes a problem. Most of it .... as fuel and livestock litter. When it is difficult to store, it .... When rice husk .... in the open or under controlled temperature in a furnace, it leaves a residue in the form of a highly reactive ash. This ash when it .... with lime, acquires cementitious properties and has the potential to replace portland cement either fully or partially in certain construction works. Scientists at the G.B. Pant University of Agriculture and Technology have developed cement from rice husk.

The cement produced from rice husk .... with sand to prepare mortar which can .... for plastering purposes, for laying bricks and stone masonry or for the construction of small houses in rural areas. The rice husk cement has a compressive strength of 30 kg/sq cm which is very low compared with that of portland cement. Rice husk cement cannot, therefore, ... for reinforced concrete constructions.

2. **Writing** — 'Cement from rice husk'

This flow chart presents the process of producing rice husk cement. Write a paragraph describing the various stages in the process of conversion of rice husk into cement. Use the flow chart and some of the words and phrases listed below for the description.

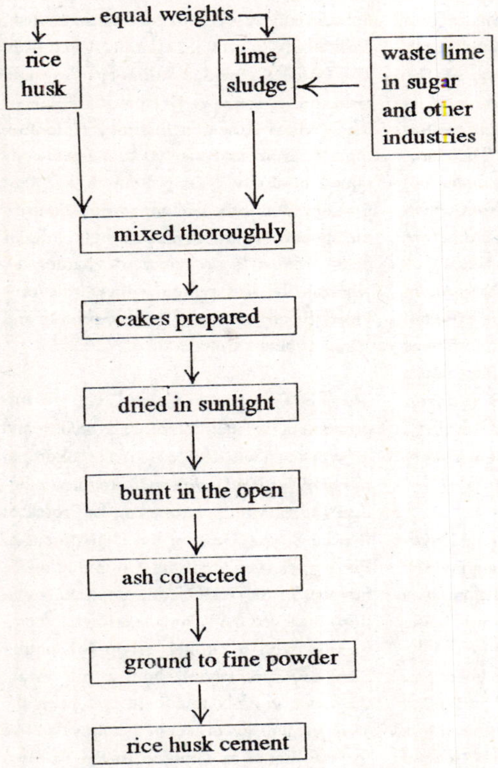

at first
initially
until
derived from
then
finally
thereafter
subsequently
on

3. **Reading** — 'Find your feet'

a. Go through the passage quickly and suggest suitable headings for the four paragraphs in the passage.

b. Read the passage in detail and answer the questions that follow it.

Leaf protein – technology to nutrition

LUNAWA is a coastal village in the southern area of Sri Lanka where the children can be seen to eat fortified *kola kenda* regularly. This local porridge traditionally made from coconut, rice and the juice from fresh green leaves, began to be repopularised by the rural development group Sarvodaya in its nursery schools during the spread of malnutrition after the 1973 cyclone. The traditional pestle and mortar was a tedious tool for the pulping of green leaves from which the juice was squeezed out by hand before including in the *kola kenda*. On hearing of Find Your Feet's work on leaf protein, Sarvodaya enquired about a more efficient juice extraction method. As many villages have no electricity, Find Your Feet had a prototype pedal-powered juice extractor made in India and commissioned it in 1982 at Lunawa, where it is still in regular daily use.

To make the leaf protein, fresh green leaves are placed into the machine through a feed hopper, and are gradually moved along by a helical screw whilst at the same time being pulped and then pressed to separate out the inedible fibre from the juice. The lower part of the cylindrical outer casing is perforated to allow the juice to be squeezed out into a container in which it is placed on a fire and heated until a coagulum forms. At this stage the pot is taken off the fire and the contents poured through a muslin bag to filter out the curd. This is washed clean with water and the resulting green product is leaf protein.

Fortified kola kenda

Adding leaf protein to the cooked rice and coconut makes fortified *kola kenda* which is nutritionally superior to the traditional dish, particularly in protein, vitamin A and iron. The fortified porridge still keeps the same taste and appearance. Dr Beatrice de Mel of the Medical Research Institute, Colombo, reported from analysis that *kola kenda* contained normally 1-2g protein in a 200ml portion. Of this the leaf juice would contribute about 0.1g protein plus about 0.25mg of beta-carotene (a precursor of vitamin A), whereas the leaf protein concentrate provided the children with 4-5g of protein and 12mg of beta-carotene.

The mothers were so pleased with the improvement in their children's health and growth that it was decided to make the preparation of fortified *kola kenda* standard practice. In January 1987 a team under Professor Priyani Soysa (Head of the Department of Paediatrics, University of Colombo, and a member of the WHO Committee on Nutrition) surveyed the Lunawa children in comparison with a similar group in another Sarvodaya pre-school about a mile away; the latter group's treatment had been the same in all respects except that they had had the traditional as opposed to the fortified *kola kenda*. The conclusion was that the Lunawa children's health was dramatically better.

(Source: *Appropriate Technology*, Vol 14)

c. Why is a pestle and mortar called a 'tedious tool'?

d. Make notes from the text using the following outline.

'kola kenda'

pestle and mortar

Find Your Feet

the process of
extraction

the nutrient value
pf 'kola kenda'

the improvement
in children's health

4. **Discussion** — 'Juice extractor in India'

Are you aware of any juice extractor manufactured in India involving appropriate technology? Discuss in groups its advantages and disadvantages.

Follow-up

1. Language check

Complete the following text, with suitable words.

Appropriate technology is a kind of .... cost technology. It has relevance to the .... background of people. It arises from local .... and uses local ...., both human and material. Its benefits go to the .... community. Rice-threshers operated by .... power and gobar .... plants are two good examples of appropriate technology.

2. Comprehension check

a. *Arrange in order the following bits of the process of working the bicycle-operated domestic pump.*

— The rear wheel now acts as a flywheel.
— Water is pumped out even at low speeds.
— The drive is transmitted from the front sprocket to the rear wheel.
— After use the clip is released and the chain is opened.
— A person sits on the bicycle seat and pedals.
— The rear wheel transmits the power through the second chain to the pump.

Now look at the third paragraph of the text on page 6 and check the correctness of your answer.

b. *Read the text 'Bicycle-operated domestic pump' on page 6 again and answer the following questions.*

i. Guess the meanings of the underlined words in the text.

ii. List the advantages of the pump.

iii. What do you understand by the expression 'stationary pedal power'?

3. **Oral practice**

In discussion with your neighbour, prepare a set of questions about 'kola kenda' using words like what, how, and why. If necessary, use the text on page 10 for the purpose. Now take it in turns to pose questions and answer. Try to speak as quickly and accurately as you can.

4. **Writing skills development**

Develop the following hints into a paragraph to describe a paddy-husk cumbustor cum heat exchanger.

> Paddy husk - considered waste - storage problem - disposal problem - its commercial use now for drying paddy in rice mills possible - A paddy-husk cumbustor cum heat exchanger developed for this purpose - device - vertical cylindrical cumbustor - heat exchanger mounted over it - main principle of its working - husk fed into the combustor - completely burned inside - hot air in heat exchanger - delivered to dryer through ducts - parboiled paddy in the dryer - dried by this means.

Technology Unit 2

Printing

Preparation

1. Language development

a. When we describe a number of actions occurring one after another, we use words that indicate the sequence: (sequence words)

first, firstly
second, secondly
then
next
after that
finally

b. *Rewrite the sentences in the following paragraph in the correct order, filling the gaps with appropriate sequence words.*

i. .... , the roller on the machine is inked, and .... , the roller is rotated either by hand or by means of an automatic device.

ii. .... corrections are carried out on the stencil paper.

iii. .... the stencil paper is placed in position on the duplicating machine.

iv. If you want to make many copies of a document or a letter, you can make use of a duplicating machine.

v. ...., the stencil paper is removed from the machine and stored for future use.

vi. This is done by painting the correcting fluid on the wrong line, allowing the fluid to dry, and .... typing the correct words over the paint.

vii. .... , the letter should be typed on stencil paper, setting the typewriter to the stencil-cutting position.

c. i. *Match the words in column A with their meanings in column B.*

A	B
type	engraving, an incised figure or design in stone and the like
offset	the art or process of putting writing or designs on stone with a greasy substance, and of producing printed impressions therefrom
intaglio	the ability to attempt something new, difficult or important
letterpress	a rectangular block usually of metal or wood, having its face so shaped as to produce, in printing, a letter, figure or other character
lithography	being out of date, no longer useful
layout	a process of printing from a flat surface in which the impression is first received by a rubber-surfaced cylinder, from which it is transferred to the paper
inventory	admitting passage of light, shining through
enterprise	reading-matter, as distinct from illustrations
obsolescence	the make-up of a page, a book, newspaper, etc
translucent	an itemised list of goods with their estimated worth

ii. *Fill in the blanks in the following passage with appropriate words from column A.*

Although there is evidence to show that some form of printng was known in ancient times, it was printing by movable .... that constituted a turning point in the development of printing. The invention of printing as we know it today is ascribed to the .... of Johann Gutenberg (1400 - 68) of Strasbourg. Another invention made in the early years of the nineteenth century was .... This method makes use of the principle of repulsion between grease and water A further advance in litho printing was made with the introduction of .... litho printing: in this method the impression on the litho plate is transferred to a rubber roller and then printed on paper. Whereas in lithography the printing plate is flat and in .... the type stands cut in relief, in .... printing the image to be printed appears as hollows recessed beneath the surface.

2. Oral practice

Work with your partner and fill in the first column of the following chart with as many examples of printed matter as you can think of. Then fill in the second and third columns against each example in the first.

examples of printed matter	purpose served	of permanent, semi-permanent or temporary value
1. handbill	making an announcement	temporary
2.		
3.		
4.		
5.		
6.		
7.		

3. Reading skills development

On the next page are the title and the first paragraph of a piece of text. Look at the title first and try to predict what the text is likely to be about. Then read the text.

Printing on its way out?

For those of us who harbour the rankling fear that the printed word is on its way out and that the electronic age is about to take over the world of books, a visit to the children's section of an American public library is a great morale booster.

i. Read the following sentence and guess the meaning of the expression morale booster .

'Receiving praise is a morale booster, but failure isn t.

ii. Why is a visit to the children's section of an American public library a morale booster?

iii. Now predict what the rest of the text is likely to do.

Part 1

1. **Reading — 'Traditional printing methods'**

a. In pairs discuss

i. what you know about the history of printing.

ii. what you know about printing processes, old and new.

b. Look at the following flow chart which describes the process of lithography in the nineteenth century.

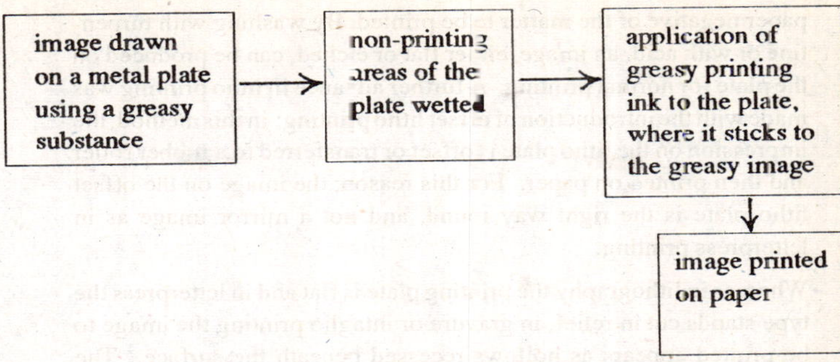

Now read the following text, *Traditional printing methods*, and check whether the information in the text about lithography in the nineteenth century is adequately represented by the flow chart given.

Although there is evidence to show that some form of printing was known in ancient times, it was printing by movable type that constituted a turning point in the development of printing. The invention of printing as we know it today is ascribed to Johann Gutenberg (1440-68) of Strasbourg. In 1456 the Gutenberg Bible, the first major printed book, appeared; it had more than 600 leaves, with two columns of 42 lines each. Typefoundry too developed side by side. The type was made by pouring molten type metal, generally an alloy of tin and lead, into a mould. Typesetting was done by hand and the types were wedged together in a tray. Ink was spread on the type and then the paper was pressed against the types. This continued to be the basic method of printing till the present day. Mechanisation began in the early years of the nineteenth century, when Friedrich Konig built a printing machine. In the early machines, the types moved first under a roller which inked them and then under a cylinder which carried the paper to be printed on.

Another invention made in the early years of the nineteenth century was lithography. This method makes use of the principle of repulsion between grease and water. In simple terms, the process consists of drawing the image to be printed on a metal plate using a greasy substance. Then the plate is wetted. The grease on the plate repels the water and consequently only the non-printing areas become wet. When greasy printing ink is applied to the plate, it sticks to the greasy image but not to the non-printing areas. From this plate, the image can be printed on paper. In photolithography the printing stone is coated with a light-sensitive substance and then exposed to light through a paper negative of the matter to be printed. By washing with turpentine or with acid, an image, either flat or etched, can be produced on the plate for normal printing. A further advance in litho printing was made with the introduction of offset litho printing: in this method, the impression on the litho plate is offset or transferred to a rubber roller and then printed on paper. For this reason, the image on the offset litho plate is the right way round, and not a mirror image as in letterpress printing.

Whereas in lithography the printing plate is flat and in letterpress the type stands cut in relief, in gravure or intaglio printing the image to be printed appears as hollows recessed beneath the surface. The lower part of the cylinder carrying the image rolls is a reservoir of ink and as it comes out, a steel blade (the doctor blade) wipes the cylinder leaving ink only in the hollows. The printing is then done on paper. If you look at the printed matter produced by gravure through a magnifying glass, you will find that the image is made up of a large number of dots. The dots will vary in size and density to produce darker or lighter areas on paper.

c. *Based on the information provided by the text, draw similar flow charts showing the following processes.*

   i. printing by movable type

   ii. photolithography or gravure printing.

2. **Listening** — 'Paper for printing'

You will now listen to a talk on paper used fo
different contexts. Listen carefully and make not
following chart.

type of paper	property	use

3. **Reading** — 'Printing engineering plans'

a. Suppose you are the manager of an engineering firm. You are thinking of buying an engineering plan printer. List the questions you would like answered first before you make the purchase. Do you think any advertisement would answer all these questions?

b. Read the advertisement on the next page for the Modi Xerox 2510 and check if it answers your questions.

c. List three reasons why would you buy this machine, and three why you would not.

Modi Xerox 2510
The Small Printer with Big Benefits

Now you can get high quality, dry black-on white size-to-size exerographic prints of all your engineering drawings and other large sized documents upto AO – including the filling strips - just at the press of a button.

The Modi Xerox 2510 is a compact Engineering Plan Printer which enables you to take prints from a wide range of originals – translucent or opaque and even rigid mounted drawings upto 3mm thick. Prints of existing prints are no more a problem and you do not have to incur the additional cost of producing translucent secondary masters, to make these copies.

No 'special' requirements

As the Modi Xerox 2510 uses the safe and completely odourless exerographic process, it can be installed at the point of need, just anywhere in your office – no more special rooms. And because it uses plain paper you can do away with the inventory of special sensitised printing material which has a limited shelf life. The Modi Xerox 2510 print speed remains constant at 3 metres per minute, irrespective of whether you are *printing on* polyester film, tracing or paper or *printing from* any type of original.
If your requirement is for prints on polyester or tracing, it is recommended, that for every 2 prints taken on either of these two materials, at least 8 prints be taken on paper, before switching back to polyester/tracing.

Assured Reliability

Readily available spares and consumables and a specially trained service force ensure that your Modi Xerox 2510 gives you copies - whenever you want them.

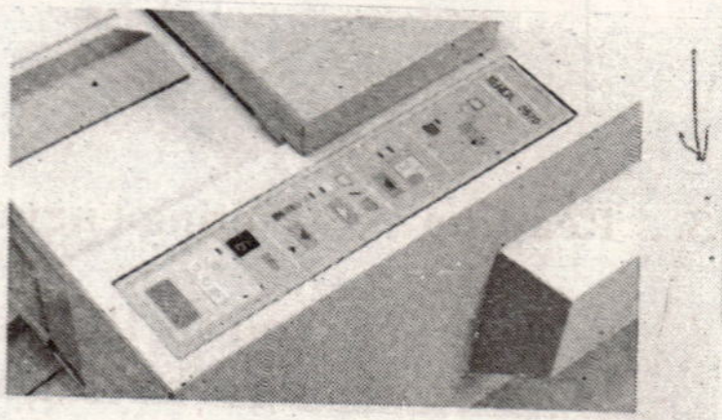

Specifications

Original Input
Minimum Size: A4.
Maximum Size: 914mm wide X 3 metres
Rigid Originals: Up to 3 mm thick.

Print Output
Manual Feed: Cut Sheets.
Minimum Size: A3 short edge feed
Maximum Size: 914mm wide X 3 metres
Print Stock: Plain paper (60-120 gsm), tracing paper (90gsm) and polyester film (100 microns)

Print Speed
All Print Output: Constant at 3 metres per minute.

Microprocessor Control Functions
- Light or dark original setting. (to reduce or eliminate unwanted background)
- Fuser temperature control. (1: bond/tracing, 2: polyester, 3: heavyweight materials)
- Print contrast control – 5 steps. (darkens or lightens image)

Status Indicators
- Power Saver Standby.
- Ready to Print (with audible signal).
- Resettable Print Counter.
- Printer Status Codes including extensive, Service Diagnostics.

Electrical Requirements
Standard single phase 15 amp. 220/240 volt power outlet.

Warm Up Time
Initial Warm Up: 80 seconds.
Power Saver Standby: 2 to 30 seconds.
Continuous Prints: Instantaneous.

Dimensions
Height: 40cms.
Width: 140cms.
Depth: 50cms.

Weight
80kg.

Modi Xerox
Setting the standards for others to copy!

Whilst this information is correct at the time of going to press, Modi Xerox reserves the right at any time to change the specifications of the equipment described herein without notice. Xerox is a registered trade mark of Rank Xerox Ltd. (U.K.) and Xerox Corpn. USA.

The introduction of these technologies has not only greatly increased productivity and printing quality but has also reduced costs.

B. **CHHABRA :** You have been in India for almost two weeks now and have visited a number of newspaper presses around the country. What are your impressions?

TROCKI : What <u>astounded</u> us was the fact that there are well over 20,000 newspapers in India — almost three times the number in the United States. Such a figure is simply <u>inconceivable</u> for us. But many Indian newspapers are news-sheets and the number of pages is also very small compared with the American papers.

The *New York Times*, for example, has 100 or more pages on Sundays.

C. **CHHABRA :** What do you think of the status of printing technology in India vis-a-vis America?

TROCKI : Compared with the United States, the printing technology in general here is quite far behind. But if it serves the needs, it may be appropriate. However, I must say that during our visits we saw some of the latest <u>state-of-the-art</u> technology in operation, particularly with national newspapers. There is certainly a noticeable trend to switch over to new technology in regional and medium-size newspapers as well.

D. **CHHABRA :** That brings me to small newspapers. Many newspapers in India are small with limited circulations and funds. Do you think the new technologies can help them? What is your experience in America?

TROCKI : Yes. One of the most important areas in which the new technology has had an impact on the small- and medium-size newspapers in America is in the prepress area, especially typesetting. Even this is now undergoing some changes as a result of the <u>advent</u> of low-cost laser printers with the <u>potential</u> to replace photographic typesetters and the availability of low cost software packages, running on personal computers capable of integrating text and graphics.

Small American newspapers have found that personal computers, such as the Apple company's Macintosh and its Laser Writer, are economical and adequate for setting up text and advertising pages, including layout. This equipment costs less than 25 per cent of the standard digital phototypesetting system.

E. CHHABRA : Mr Eddings, you have first-hand experience with the new technology. Would you say that personal computers and laser printers do as good a job as a phototypesetter?

EDDINGS : They don't give you the quality that phototypesetters do, but for the needs of small newspapers they are quite adequate. More important than quality, what small newspapers need most is the ability to produce their papers quickly, efficiently and economically. In any case, one must remember that most small newspapers are produced on newsprint which does not give high quality.

Another important advantage of personal computers is that, contrary to common belief, they are very easy to operate; they require minimum training. One can train anyone with some basic intelligence to use these machines in days compared with the years of step-by-step training needed for conventional printing technology. Offset presses still require a rigorous training regimen. but personal computers don't ...

F. CHHABRA : Many owners of small newspapers in India have very limited funds; they still do hand composing with a few people on a letterpress. Do you still think it will be worth their while to invest in this new equipment?

EDDINGS : They are the best judge of what is good for them. But the big advantage of the new technology, personal computers and laser printers in America is that it is quite reasonably priced. I hope it will be priced that way in India also; ultimately I think it will be. The technology lends itself to easy replacement. For example, if a Macintosh computer terminal breaks down in my office and I cannot get it fixed, I can always replace the terminal for what I consider a very reasonable price. No one ever replaced a typesetter inexpensively.

G. CHHABRA : This new technology is adequate for typesetting, and I understand that by next year it may be possible to have these computers with capabilities to typeset Indian languages, but what about printing?

EDDINGS : It is fairly obvious to me that the investment required to purchase any press is huge. Ultimately, no matter what kind of company one has, the decision to buy a press is a major financial decision. It seems to me that the small newspaper owners in India may find themselves in the same situation that Americans do: they do not own a press, but buy time on someone else's press. You do not have to own a press to put out a newspaper. You can take your camera-ready copy to the market-place to have it printed.

If I were to give any kind of message to printers and publishers here in India, I would say: Don't be afraid of technological change. Whether you like it nor not, it will ultimately come. So the earlier you switch over, the better.

i. List the changes in the American newspaper printing and publishing industry in recent times under the following headings :

   a. areas of change
   b. effects

ii. What are the differences between Indian and American newspapers?

iii. What does Eddings mean when he says 'you do not have to own a press to put out a newspaper'?

iv. Look back at the passage and try to guess the meanings of the underlined words from the context or from their forms. If you cannot, ask your neighbour.

2. **Writing** — 'Help small Indian newspapers survive!'

Imagine that you are the President of the Association of Small Newspapers in India. Write a letter to the Government of India stating the problems faced by small newspapers in India and suggesting ways in which the Government of India could help in the matter. If necessary, discuss the issue with your partner before writing.

3. **Reading** — 'Printing on its way out?'

a. Discuss with your partner if the reading habit among children today is on the decline. Also discuss the factors supporting your conclusions.

b. Read the first paragraph of the following text and answer the question which follows it immediately. Then read the second paragraph and similarly answer the question which follows it immediately. Now read the rest of the text and then answer the questions at the end of it.

For those of us who harbour the rankling fear that the printed word is on its way out and that the electronic age is about to take over the world of books, a visit to the children's section of an American public library is a great morale booster.

(You have just read the first paragraph of the text. What do you expect the text to do?)

It has often been said that electronic media, such as television and videocassette recorders, and, indeed, the computer itself with its special language, will soon render our children illiterate as far as the printed word goes, while our own reliance on reading will hasten our obsolescence. It did appear for a time during the 1950s and 1960s in America that children were becoming mesmerised by the images on the television screen to the exclusion of all else, and a good deal of time, effort and money went into researching the probable outcome of what seemed to be a near-total enslavement.

(The second paragraph also refers to the fears that the author finds among people. Are these fears different from the fear mentioned in the first paragraph? The paragraph uses the words ***our own*** *('while our own reliance .....'). Who is referred to by the word* ***our****? What is the enslavement mentioned at the end of the paragraph?)*

Now that the United States is well into its third generation of television watchers, who are more than ever surrounded by high-tech wonders, it appears that earlier fears were unwarranted; it simply has not come to pass that children turned their backs on books.

That they have not, that books in America especially children's books are being produced in greater number today than ten years ago is due in great part to the enterprise of the public libraries in the United States. These have been in existence in some form or another since colonial times and have enjoyed legal status for more than 100 years; but it has only been since the 1920s that they began diversifying their services, and, as a start, opened up special departments for children.

It was about that time also when the American Library Association (ALA) began giving more importance to children's books and, among other activities, established the Newbery and Caldecott awards, the prestigious annual prizes for excellence in writing and illustration respectively, for juveniles. All this has led to librarians' taking a greater interest in the processes that bring about the production and distribution of books for children, and to reviewers and critics' taking more seriously the quality of these books. The active encouragement of the ALA has also stimulated many first-rate adult-book writers to turn their talents to writing for children.

Meanwhile, the new media have come to stay. They occupy space beside the book collections and enhance the library's basic function as a repository for the culture and recorded history of mankind. However, the primacy of the printed word remains intact.

i. List the measures mentioned in the text which encouraged the production of children's books.

ii. What evidence do you find in the text to support the inference that the electronic media and the printed word co-exist?

iii. Do you agree that it is the author's opinion that books continue to be read? Cite two statements in the text that express this opinion in a categorical way.

iv. What would you now like the author to tell you about American children's continuing interest in reading?

> **Learner awareness**
> You have learnt to practise the art of predicting the gist of a text as well as the organisation of its parts. The ability to predict helps you read a text with confidence and ease. Make it a habit, therefore, to predict as often as you can for making reading successful.

Follow-up

1. Oral practice

Look at the last three sections of the specifications about the Modi Xerox 2510 on page 22. Working in pairs prepare a list of questions based on the specifications about the dimensions, weight and electrical requirements of the equipment such as 'What is the height of the equipment?' or 'How much does the equipment weigh?' When you are ready, take it in turns to ask and answer questions. Be clear and accurate while speaking.

2. **Comprehension check**

Guess the meaning of the words underlined in the following passage from their context.

The active encouragement of the American Library Association has <u>stimulated</u> many first-rate adult-book writers to turn their talents to writing for children. Meanwhile, the new electronic media have come to stay. They occupy space beside the book collections and <u>enhance</u> the library's basic function as a <u>repository</u> for the culture and recorded history of mankind. However, the <u>primacy</u> of the printed word remains <u>intact</u>.

3. **Language check**

Fill in the blanks in the following passage with appropriate words.

> Newspaper printing and publishing in the United States had undergone a complete .... in the past twenty years, first by the .... of electronic and computer typesetting, and .... by the change-over from letterpress to offset lithography. More .... 80 per cent of all daily .... in America are now printed by offset.
>
> Both electronics and computers have greatly advanced printing ....

Now check your answer with your neighbour's.

4. **Writing skills development**

Look at the chart you made while doing the listening task on page 21. Using the chart write a paragraph about the properties and uses of the different types of paper involved in printing.

Technology Unit 3

Evaluating technology

Evaluating technology

Preparation

1. Language development

Guess the meanings of the words underlined in the following passages from their context. Consult your neighbour, if necessary.

a. The community-type hybrid solar cooker consists of a wooden box with a steel tray inside. The tray is painted black and covered with glass sheets which accounts for the quick heat trap. The black paint and the insulation prevent the heat from escaping. The cumulative heat built up inside the wooden box accelerates the cooking of food items kept in the aluminium utensils.

b. This unit can be used for cooking a large quantity of food (e.g. for noon-meal schemes in schools). Conventional fuel is saved by 40 per cent. The disadvantage is that even though three or four items of food can be cooked simultaneously, depending upon the size of the box, the cooking has to be done in the open. This project was proved to be economically viable after several experiments.

c. The import of technology at prohibitive costs has the disadvantages of widening the gap between the rich and the poor, effecting cultural distortion imposing alien cultural trends and patterns of consumption on the local public, perpetuating technological dependence on others and discarding traditional technology.

2. Reading skills development

You will find on page 34 the first sentences of a few paragraphs. Read them and then try to guess what the rest of each paragraph is likely to be about.

a. Most people imagine that technology can only bring happiness and prosperity to the people of the world.

b. What has been said about technology in general so far is also true of Indian technology.

c. Modern technology has become very much an integral part of our existence.

d. There was once a town in the heart of America where all life seemed to live in harmony with its surroundings.

Check your answers with your neighbour's.

3. Oral practice

Technology has conferred a number of benefits on mankind. At the same time, it has created some problems, too. Discuss these with your partner and make two lists, one of benefits and another of problems resulting from technology.

4. Writing skills development

Use your lists to write a paragraph either on the benefits of technology or on the problems created by it.

Part 1

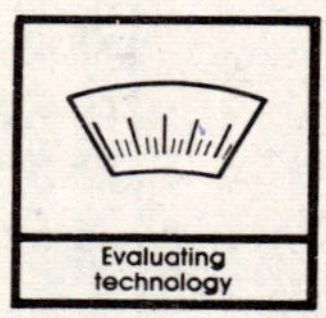

1. Discussion — 'Solar energy'

Today solar energy is being seriously considered as an alternative to energy from oil. Can you say why?

Compare with another student the features of solar energy with those of energy from oil. The following questions will help you to make the comparison.

a. Will this form of energy run out? That is, will it be used up, and then not be available in the future?

b. Can we get a regular supply of this form of energy? (Think of winter, and of cloudy days.)

c. Are transport and distribution costs high?

d. Can the energy be stored and tapped when required?

Now here are some more facts about solar energy. Discuss them with your partner and decide whether they are advantages or drawbacks.

e. The photovoltaic cell can directly convert solar energy into electricity.

f. Photovoltaic technology is expensive.

g. Some large international corporations are turning solar energy into a high-tech industry.

h. Solar energy can be used to supplement fossil fuels and thus save them for peak periods of demand.

2. **Reading** — 'Hybrid solar cooker'

a. By looking at the title of the text, try to guess what the text is likely to deal with.

b. Read the text and check whether your guess is correct.

c. Answer the questions that follow the text.

Hybrid Solar Cooker

From the economic point of view, solar cookers are ideal cooking devices for rural India. But when one considers the time factor, they prove to be very disappointing. Ordinary solar cookers are best suited for foods that require long slow boiling such as stews, cereals and vegetables.

This 'Community-Type Hybrid Solar Cooker' was designed bearing in mind both cost and time as the two main deciding factors. The special feature of this cooking device is that the heat energy trapped by flat plate collectors can be supplemented by burning coal or other conventional fuels. This makes it more appropriate for traditional cooking in rural areas.

This cooker consists of three main parts:

a. a wooden box
b. a steel tray painted black and covered with glass sheets
c. an insulated upper lid with glass plates.

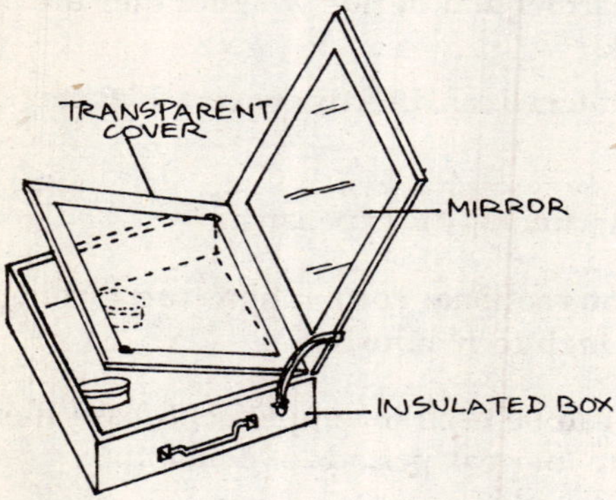

The steel tray, which is fixed inside the box, is painted black and covered with glass sheets which accounts for the quick heat trap. The black paint and the insulation prevent the heat from escaping. The cumulative heat built up inside the wooden box accelerates the cooking of food items kept in the aluminium utensils. Aluminium utensils are also coated black and they are placed on the absorbing surfaces for cooking.

This hybrid system permits the gas produced by burning fuel in a grate to be drawn into the box through a duct under the absorber plate by natural draft which is made possible by a chimney.

The advantage of this unit is that it can be used on cloudy as well as sunny days. The combination of conventional fuels and solar energy saves 60 per cent of the cooking time. This unit can be used for cooking a large quantity of food (e.g. for noon-meal schemes in schools). Conventional fuel is saved by 40 per cent. The disadvantage is that even though three or four items of food can be cooked simultaneously, depending upon the size of the box, the cooking has to be done in the open. This project was proved to be economically viable after experiments.

i. What is the problem with ordinary solar cookers?

ii. What is the special feature of the hybrid solar cooker?

iii. Which aspects of the cooker help it trap the heat?

iv. What are the four main advantages of this type of cooker?

v. What is its disadvantage?

3. Language focus — 'Advertisements'

Look at the two Larsen and Toubro advertisements on the following pages. Pay attention to the way in which language is used in the two advertisements. Answer the following questions.

a. Both the advertisements are by the same company. Are the products advertised the same?

b. Which advertisement do you find easy to understand? Can you guess why?

c. Look at the words used: mark the technical words used in two advertisements. Which one uses more technical words?

d. Look at the sentences. Which one uses longer sentences?

e. One of the advertisements uses a large number of 'incomplete' sentences, which consist only of clauses or phrases. Mark such sentences.

f. Which advertisement contains more statements of fact?

g. Look at the adjectives. Which advertisement has more adjectives in the superlative degree (words like *biggest*, *best* and in the comparative degree?

h. One of the advertisements is addressed to engineers, and the other to non-specialists, perhaps to managers. Do you agree? Look at the answers to questions (b) to (f) and find evidence for this statement.

i. Look at the use of pronouns in the advertisements. Which one uses first and second person pronouns (*we*, *you*)?

j. Which advertisement sounds the more personal of the two? What makes it personal? What makes the other impersonal and formal? (Try to guess the meaning of the word 'formal', or ask your teacher.)

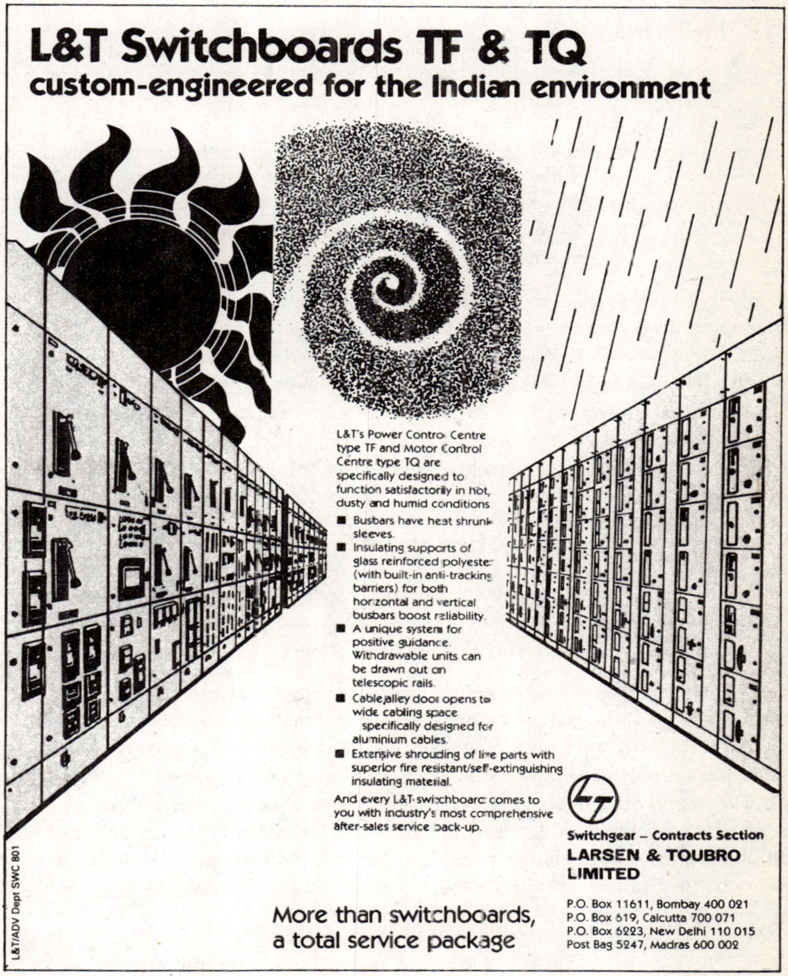
L&T Switchboards TF & TQ
custom-engineered for the Indian environment
L&T's Power Control Centre type TF and Motor Control Centre type TQ are specifically designed to function satisfactorily in hot, dusty and humid conditions
Busbars have heat shrunk sleeves.
Insulating supports of glass reinforced polyester (with built-in anti-tracking barriers) for both horizontal and vertical busbars boost reliability.
A unique system for positive guidance. Withdrawable units can be drawn out on telescopic rails.
Cable alley door opens to wide cabling space specifically designed for aluminium cables.
Extensive shrouding of live parts with superior fire resistant/self-extinguishing insulating material.
And every L&T-switchboard comes to you with industry's most comprehensive after-sales service back-up.
Switchgear – Contracts Section
LARSEN & TOUBRO LIMITED
P.O. Box 11611, Bombay 400 021
P.O. Box 619, Calcutta 700 071
P.O. Box 6223, New Delhi 110 015
Post Bag 5247, Madras 600 002
More than switchboards, a total service package
L&T/ADV Dept SWC 801

4. **Reading** — 'Technology: benefits and drawbacks'

Read the text below. Pause while you read, and answer the questions given.

Most people imagine that technology by itself can bring happiness and prosperity to the people of the world ...

---

a. From the first sentence, what do you guess to be the subject of the text that follows?

b. If you have to write about the subject in three paragraphs, what will you include in each of the three paragraphs? Discuss this with your neighbour and outline a plan. Come back to this question after reading the text and compare your answer with the contents of the text.

But really technology is a mixed package; it has its benefits and its disadvantages. Technology is the power derived from the application of knowledge. This power has been sought to be utilised to improve the standards of living of people all over the world. It cannot be denied that advances in technology have had a tremendously beneficial impact on food production, health care, housing, education, transport, communication and other important sectors of life. Human life has been rendered easier and more comfortable thanks to technology.

---

c. Science is defined as 'knowledge arranged in an orderly manner'. How does technology differ from science?

d. What is the main point made in this paragraph? From your answers to questions (a) and (b), what do you expect the next paragraph to be about?

Turning to the other side of the picture, we find that technology has led to pollution of the environment. The concentration of human and material resources at a few centres has resulted in large-scale migration of rural population to urban areas and the consequent problems of urbanisation and slums, problems economic as well as social. The import of technology at prohibitive costs has the additional disadvantages of widening the gap between the rich and the poor, effecting cultural distortions, imposing alien cultural trends and patterns of consumption on the local public, perpetuating technological dependence on others and discarding traditional technology.

---

e. Which of the following statements are true?

- As a result of technology, people in villages are leading contented lives.
- Technology has solved the problems resulting from urbanisation.

- Technology has narrowed the difference between the rich and the poor.
- New technology has driven out old technology.

What has been said about technology in general so far is also true of Indian technology. Notwithstanding the label 'developing country', today India is a technical power to reckon with among the nations of the world. Great strides of progress have been made in the fields of railways, telecommunication, power generation, steel, oil, chemicals and fertilizers, and food production. At the same time the industrial slums of New Delhi, Calcutta, Bombay and Madras with their attendant problems are a stern reminder of the drawbacks of technology. Similarly, the ghastly tragedy that recently overtook the residents of Bhopal as a result of toxic gas escaping from the Union Carbide plant is a ready instance of the hazards posed by technology.

---

f. This is the third paragraph of the text. How does it differ from the third paragraph of your plan in question (b) above?

g. This paragraph refers to two drawbacks of technology. Can you find words or phrases referring to these drawbacks in the previous paragraph?

Modern technology has become very much a part of our existence, so that we cannot do without it, even if we want to. Particularly in areas where mass production is involved and where issues of national prestige and security are at stake, advanced modern technology may be the only answer. However, it is advisable not to depend on imported technology but to develop indigenous technology wherever possible. This must be so, particularly keeping in mind the fact that there is a vast labour force available in India and that most of the people in India live in villages and semi-urban centres.

---

h. Only one of the following statements is true according to the paragraph. Find it.
- The author says that technology is evil and we must give it up.
- The author says that technology brings us so many benefits that we must pursue it.
- The author says that technology is an indispensable necessity and we have to use it.

---

i. Why does the author recommend the use of indigenous technology in India?

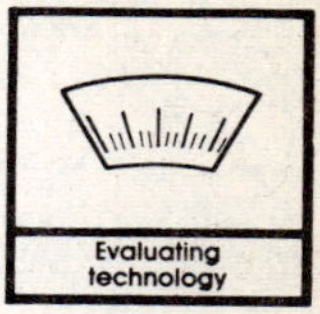

Part 2

1. **Reading** — 'A fable for tomorrow'

Silent Spring

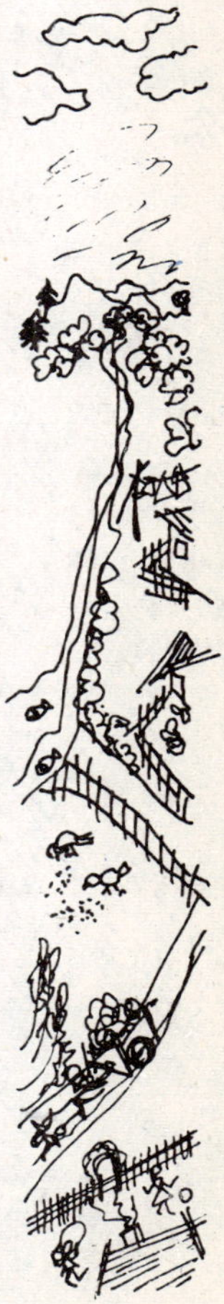

There was once a town in the heart of America where all life seemed to live in harmony with its surroundings. The town lay in the midst of a checkerboard of prosperous farms, with fields of grain and hillsides of orchards where, in spring, white clouds of bloom drifted above the green fields. In autumn, oak and maple and birch set up a blaze of colour that flamed and flickered across a backdrop of pines. Then foxes barked in the hills and deer silently crossed the fields, half hidden in the mists of the fall mornings.

Along the roads, laurel, viburnum and alder, great ferns and wildflowers delighted the traveller's eye through much of the year. Even in winter the roadsides were places of beauty, where countless birds came to feed on the berries and on the seed heads of dried weeds rising above the snow. The countryside was, in fact, famous for the abundance and variety of its bird life, and when the flood of migrants was pouring through in spring and fall, people travelled from great distances to observe them. Others came to fish in the streams which flowed clear and cold out of the hills and contained shady pools where trout lay. So it had been from the days many years ago when the first settlers raised their houses, sank their wells and built their barns.

Then a strange blight crept over the area and everything began to change. Some evil spell had settled on the community: mysterious maladies swept the flocks of chickens: the cattle and sheep sickened and died. Everywhere there was a shadow of death. The

farmers spoke of much illness among their families. In the town the doctors had become more and more puzzled by new kinds of sickness appearing among their patients. There had been several sudden and unexplained deaths, not only among adults but even among children, who would be stricken suddenly while at play and die within a few hours.

There was a strange stillness. The birds, for example — where had they gone? Many people spoke of them, puzzled and disturbed. The feeding stations in the backyards were deserted. The few birds seen anywhere were moribund; they trembled violently and could not fly. It was a spring without voices. The mornings that had once throbbed with the dawn chorus of robins, catbirds, doves, jays, wrens, and scores of other bird voices, there was now no sound; only silence lay over the fields and woods and marsh.

On the farms the hens brooded, but no chicks hatched. The farmers complained that they were unable to raise any pigs — the litters were small and the young survived only a few days. The apple trees were coming into bloom but no bees droned among the blossoms, so there was no pollination and there would be no fruit.

The roadsides, once so attractive, were now lined with browned and withered vegetation as though swept by fire. These, too, were silent, deserted by all living things. Even the streams were now lifeless. Anglers no longer visited them, for all the fish had died.

In the gutters under the eaves and between the shingles of the roofs, a white granular powder still showed a few patches; some weeks before it had fallen like snow upon the roofs and the lawns, the fields and streams.

No witchcraft, no enemy action had silenced the rebirth of new life in this stricken world. The people had done it themselves.

This town does not actually exist, but it might easily have a thousand counterparts in America or elsewhere in the world. I know of no community that has experienced all the misfortunes I describe. Yet every one of these disasters has actually happened somewhere, and many real communities have already suffered a substantial number of them. A grim spectre has crept upon us almost unnoticed, and this imagined tragedy may easily become a stark reality we shall all know.

Rachel Carson
Silent Spring, 1962

After reading the story, *Silent Spring,* answer the following questions.

a. The author's main purpose in writing this story is
— to entertain readers.
— to present important information.
— to give a warning.

b. Look at the organisation of the writing. Can you divide the text into three parts?
Point out the place where the author moves from one part to the next.

Evaluating technology

c. Which paragraph describes the colours of spring? Which paragraph describes the sounds of spring?

d. Guess the meanings of the following phrases, with the help of another student, if necessary:
— checkerboard of farms
— white clouds of bloom
— backdrop of pines
— mists of the fall morning

e. What happened to
the birds ?
the farmers' relatives?
the town's children ?
the apple blossom?

f. The words 'science' and 'technology' are not used in the story. Find a place in the story where the author seems to refer indirectly to science and technology.

g. Find the phrases used by the author (in paragraphs 3, 8 and 9) to describe the 'tragedy'.

h. How does the author argue that these are not imaginary sufferings?

i. Read the first sentence of the fable again. How does it describe life in early days in America? Rewrite the sentence, using some of the same words with necessary modifications, to describe life in the same American town after the tragedy.

2. **Language focus** — 'Policy on technology'

The Government of India has issued a Technology Policy Statement in which the aims of India's technology policy have been spelt out. Some of these aims are listed below. Make seven sentences beginning with 'India's technology policy tries to ... , and putting together three appropriate items, one from each of the following three columns.

India's technology policy tries to ...

A	B	C
— provide the maximum gainful and satisfying employment to all strata of society		improve the quality of the habitat
— ensure maximum development	particularly	those with export potential
— develop technologies which are internationally competitive	and	make full utilisation of by-products
— ensure the correct mix between mass production technologies	with	emphasis on employment of women and weaker sections of society

— reduce demands on energy	production by the masses
— ensure harmony with the environment	minimum capital outlay
— recycle waste material	energy from non-renewable sources

3. **Reading** — 'Mass production or production by the masses?'

a. Look at the title of the text and try to guess what the text is likely to deal with.

b. *Read the following paragraph and answer the question that follows.*

> As Gandhi said, the poor of the world cannot be helped by mass production, only by production by the masses. The system of mass production, based on sophisticated, highly capital-intensive, high energy-input dependent, and human labour-saving technology, presupposes that you are already rich, for a great deal of capital investment is needed to establish one single workplace. The system of production by the masses mobilises the priceless resources which are possessed by all human beings, their clever brains and skilful hands, and supports them with first-class tools. The technology of mass production is inherently violent, ecologically damaging, self-defeating in terms of non-renewable resources, and stultifying for the human person. The technology of production by the masses, making use of the best of modern knowledge and experience, is conducive to decentralisation, compatible with the laws of ecology, gentle in its use of scarce resources, and designed to serve the human person instead of making him the servant of human machines. I have named it intermediate technology to signify that it is vastly superior to the primitive technology of bygone ages but at the same time much simpler, cheaper and freer than the super-technology of the rich. One can also call it self-help technology, or democratic or people's technology — a technology to which everybody can gain admittance and which is not reserved to those already rich and powerful.

E.R. Schumacher
Small is Beautiful, 1973.

Using the information contained in the text, complete the following sentences to bring out the differences between the two types of technology.

a. Mass production requires a heavy investment of capital, *but* ....

b. .... ; mass production, *on the other hand*, uses sophisticated machines and instruments.

c. *Whereas* mass production makes use of labour-saving technology, ...

d. *While* mass production does violence to ecology, ...

e. .... the servant of machines. .... *in contrast*, ...

f. In mass production technology, non-renewable resources .... In Gandhian technology, ...

g. Intermediate technology is .... primitive technology. *At the same time*, it is .... mass production technology.

h. Whereas mass production technology is reserved .... , people's technology ....

4. **Writing** — 'An Indian village a hundred years from now'

It is sometime towards the end of the twentyfirst century. Imagine you are living in an Indian village. Write a paragraph describing what the village looks like under the impact of technology over the years.

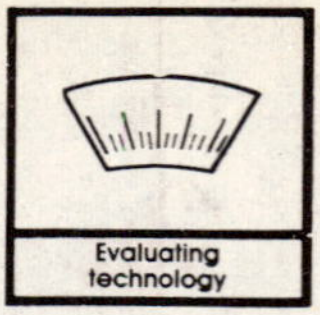

Follow-up

1. Comprehension check

Read the text 'Mass production or production by the masses?' on page 136 again and say which of the following statements are true and which are false. Correct the false statements.

a. Production by the masses is production of goods on a large scale, employing sophisticated technology.

b. Mass production is highly capital-intensive.

c. Production by the masses makes use of human resources, employing intermediate technology.

d. Mass production is the technology of the poor.

e. Production by the masses is not reserved only for the rich and the powerful.

f. The technology of production by the masses is harmful to ecology.

2. Language check

Complete the following passage by filling in the blanks with appropriate words.

Technology is a mixed package; it has its benefits and its .... Technology is the .... derived from the application of knowledge. This power has been sought to be utilised to improve the .... of living of people all over the world. It cannot be denied that advances in technology have had a tremendously beneficial .... on food production, health care, housing, education, transport, communication and other important

.... of life. Technology has made human life more comfortable. Turning to the other side of the picture, we find that technology has led to the.................................. of the environment. The concentration of human and material resources at a few centres has resulted in large-scale .... of rural population to urban areas and the consequent .... of urbanisation and slums.

Check your answer with your neighbour's.

3. Oral practice

Use the information in the passage above to ask and answer questions on the beneficial and harmful effects of technology on human life. Work with your neighbour.

4. Writing skills development

Write a paragraph outlining a specific problem faced by Indian technology, and suggesting a solution.

You could write about	lack of energy supply, lack of investment, unemployment resulting from new technology, hazards to the environment etc

When you have finished, exchange paragraphs with your neighbour and comment on each other's work.

Environment Unit 1

Pollution

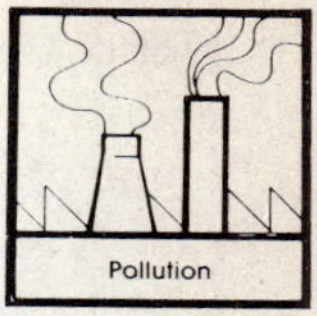

Preparation

1. Language development

a. When a word has more than one syllable, one of the syllables is uttered with greater force than the others. This is called *stress*. Here are some examples :

oxi da tion	se cu ri ty	con crete
at mos phere	un der stand	pol lu tion
de ve lop	e co lo gy	sup port
foun da tion	ma te rial	re mo val
pro duc tion	sul phu ric	in for ma tion
tem pe ra ture	ve lo ci ty	ad van ta geous
cor ro sion	mag ne tic	de gree
		dis po sal

Learn to pronounce the words correctly.
Find out how stress is marked in your dictionary.

b. Some words are differently stressed in different uses.

Read the following sentences aloud :

i a. The OBject is placed at a distance of 10 cm from the lens.

i b. I obJECT to the member's remarks.

ii a. The SUBject of my talk is 'Pollution .

ii b. As a test the metal was subJECTed to great heat.

iii a. The PROject was implemented last year.

iii b. We can proJECT the picture on a screen.

iv a. That is the PERfect solution.

iv b. The design was perFECTed after years of effort.

Notice the difference in stress of the words when used as noun and as verb.

Some other words of this type are *conduct, contract, contrast, export, rebel, produce, record*. Work in pairs to produce pairs of sentences for these words. Read them aloud to each other.

2. Writing skills development

The sentences below form a paragraph. Read the first sentence (i). Then for each of the sentences which follow, select from the pairs of sentences given: look for clues in vocabulary or meaning. Then write the sentences in the correct order. Work in pairs.

i. Automobiles constitute one of the major sources of pollution in cities.

ii a. Cars, lorries, motor-bikes speed along the roads and often cause accidents.

ii b. The gases coming out of the exhaust pipes of automobiles contain carbon monoxide and other harmful products.

iii a. Exhaust gases poison the air we breathe and people who are exposed to such gases can suffer from diseases of the lungs.

iii b. Electric cars, however, do not produce carbon monoxide.

iv a. Exhaust fumes can also produce smog, which sometimes makes visibility poor on roads and on runways in airports.

iv b. Exhaust fumes are very hot since they come out of very hot engines.

v a. Another kind of pollution caused by automobiles is noise pollution.

v b. Smog means smoke plus fog: another example is motel which is from 'motorist's hotel'.

vi a. This is caused mainly by the horns of buses and lorries, the loud noise of engines and the high-pitched sound of motor-bikes.

vi b. Loudspeakers are responsible for the noise pollution in our cities.

vii a. Thus air pollution and noise pollution are serious problems in our cities.

vii b. Loud speakers are found everywhere in our cities.

3. **Listening skills development**

You will now listen to a talk on detergents and pollution. As you listen take notes in the outline given below.

i. Disadvantages of soaps : ....
....

.... of detergents : ....
....

ii. Problems caused by detergents :

a. .... of surfactants : ....
....
....

b. .... of .... : ....
....
....

In the USA : ....
....
....

c. .... : ....
....
....

iii. ....
....

Part 1

1. **Reading** – 'Cleaning the Cooum'

   a. From the title guess what the text is likely to deal with. Discuss this with your partner and make a list of three or four themes likely to figure in it.

   b. Now read the text and compare your list with it.

   c. Make brief notes using the following framework:

      i. Description of the present state of the Cooum.

      ii. Its effect on the people of Madras

      iii. Ways of solving the problem posed by the Cooum

      iv. Difficulties involved in the process.

Cleaning the Cooum

The 18-kilometre stretch of the Cooum river today poses a serious health hazard to the people of Madras. Over the years the Cooum has been polluted with sewage discharge from more than 150 points, industrial effluents, cowdung, sullage and garbage.

'Our time is running out,' says Deborah Thiagarajan, regional convenor of the Indian National Trust for Art and Cultural Heritage (INTACH), Tamil Nadu. This American resident of Madras has been actively spearheading a novel awareness campaign to focus attention on the deteriorating condition of the river. We are five minutes to midnight in our environment crisis. We have to organise for action and awareness now.'

' The Cooum is an ecologically dead river,' says Paul Appaswamy, who holds a PhD in environmental planning fron the University of Michigan and is now a visiting fellow at th Madras Institute of Development Studies (MIDS). Jayapau Azariah, the head of the department of zoology in the Univer sity of Madras, concurs with this opinion wholeheartedly o the basis of the many studies he had conducted. Cleaning th Cooum is a project that is dear to Azariah's heart, for he sti remembers the days, some thirty years ago, when he used t swim and bathe in the river. 'I would not dream of doing now. I would probably die!'

Azariah and his department have been collecting data on tl Cooum since 1975. 'It is an oxygen-deficit river. It ge polluted in less than 15 days after the monsoons flush the rive out which only means one thing — that the river has lost it rejuvenating capacity. The Cooum is therefore rich in bacteri — it is a reservoir of infection.' A breeding ground for mos quitoes, the Cooum is often blamed for various day-to-da ailments and the outbreak and recurrence of chronic disease like malaria, jaundice, gastroenteritis, skin allergies, conjunc tivitis and respiratory problems.

However, there is now hope for the Cooum — and Madras — thanks to the efforts of Thiagarajan, a determined and spiritec American woman.

Thiagarajan's approach to the problem is quintessentially American. 'One reason we took up the Cooum project is because as an American, I have seen enough projects achieve success through community involvement. If something has to be done, take the people with you. Schemes that have failed are those that organisations have taken over, divorcing the human element from them. In the United States, the government even publishes and distributes free books giving exact instructions on how people can organise themselves to combat certain issues where the government has not been effective.

Deborah Thiagarajan has immense faith in the redeeming power of human involvement. When the Citizens for Clean Waterways (CCW), initiated by INTACH in Madras, launched its drive to collect one million signatures with a minimum voluntary donation of one rupee per person, it was an exercise, she says, in identifying 'one million people who care.'

Slowly, the Cooum has become not just a river that needed to be cleaned so a city may live, but a banner under which to rally together a people to fight for a better and cleaner environment and 'a vehicle to enlighten the citizens as to their responsibilities'.

The Cooum needs not just a cosmetic face-lift, but 'a blend of engineering, technology and bio-technology,' says Azariah.

In a layman's terms, the technical difficulty is in keeping the river mouth open. One way to do it is to manually remove the sand bar as and when it forms. This would also provide employment for people. The mechanical device used for this operation, the sand pump, has proved ineffective as it keeps breaking down; sand particles are corrosive and damage the pump.

The state government has already initiated a Rs 51 million plan for pumping seawater into the Cooum to flush out its stagnant waters and replenish their oxygen content. But, as Appaswamy points out, there is a running debate on how effective flushing operations would be. 'The effect will not be felt beyond a certain point on Commander-in-Chief Road, which is not even the halfway point,' he says.

The project to clean the Cooum is riddled with hurdles. Says Thiagarajan, 'The questions are complex. Huge costs are involved. Who will pay? What technology is most appropriate in India? The Western model is high-cost and high-tech. Indian universities should perhaps devote more time to research into efficient indigenous solutions. We have the talent, the manpower.'

While the engineers and technocrats battle with how best to clean the river, Thiagarajan is busy educating the people about the need to be involved in projects like this. She tirelessly takes the environment ethic and message to villages and schools, telling adults and children, in her faltering Tamil, about *urimai* (rights) and *kadamai* (responsibilities), impressing upon them that they are perfectly within their rights to demand water and air, but keeping them clean is 'their responsibility too, as it is everyone else's.'

(Source: *Span*)

d. Can you suggest other ways of solving the problem, not mentioned in the text?

2. **Role play** — 'Cleaning the Cooum'

Hold a meeting to discuss what can be done to clean the Cooum. By the end of your meeting, you should have a concrete proposal.

Student A: You are a zoologist from the University of Madras. You are convinced that the situation calls for a solution based on engineering, technology and biotechnology.

Student B: You are an American resident of Madras. You hope to get over the problem through community involvement.

Student C: You are the representative of the Tamil Nadu Government. You feel the state government has been already doing something to improve the situation. However, you are conscious of the limitations under which the government is functioning.

Before you hold the meeting, spend five minutes preparing what you will say. Make use of the text, 'Cleaning the Cooum', if necessary, for the purpose.

3. **Writing** — 'Report on the meeting'

Imagine that you were present at the meeting between the Zoologist, the American resident of Madras and the representative of the Tamil Nadu Government. Write a brief report on what transpired at the meeting. Begin like this:

> A meeting was held to consider measures to clean the Cooum, at ...

4. **Language focus** — 'Noise pollution in Madras'

Fill in the blanks in the following passage with appropriate words.

From a study made of the problem of noise pollution in Madras, it was seen that the sources of noise that people considered most annoying were the following:

a. automobiles
b. loudspeakers
c. aeroplanes
d. radios and stereo systems

According to the .... collected, the number of automobiles in the city had doubled in the last six years. The increase was more pronounced in heavy vehicles like buses and lorries. The vehicles were .... with air horns or other high-pitched horns which could cause great .... to hearing. Even in the vicinity of schools and hospitals, the horns were used indiscriminately. Besides the horns, the engines of many heavy commercial .... contributed to the noise pollution. Many motor-bikes had no .... and were seen tearing through the streets at high speeds.

The second source of .... was the loudspeaker. Many places of worship, of all religions, used loudspeakers to .... religious music or religious chants. During certain months, the music was played every day from 4:00 a.m. Housewives and old persons .... in the neighbourhood complained most about this noise. Another occasion when loudspeakers were .... was a wedding. Film songs were played from dawn .... well past midnight, and the songs were repeated so often.................... people reached the end of their patience.

Loudspeakers were also used at political meetings, and here again the noise continued till midnight. Very powerful loudspeakers were used and they were directed at residential .... The meeting itself was preceded by two or three hours of film songs.

The third source was the aeroplane. This complaint came

mainly from residential areas near the ....,
though some headmasters and principals complained that the planes took .... in the direction of their institutions, and classes were ....

There were a few complaints from people living in flats that their neighbours played their .... and stereo systems at high .... even late in the ....

Part 2

1. **Reading** — 'Chemical pollution and the greenhouse effect'

   a. *Discuss the following in small groups.*

      i. What is meant by the greenhouse effect?

      ii. What is the connection between ozone and ultra-violet radiation?

      iii. What are the effects of ultraviolet radiation?

      iv. What should be done to prevent ozone depletion?

   b. *Now read the following text and compare your answers to (a) with it.*

Chemical pollution is changing the structure of the earth's atmosphere resulting in the greenhouse effect and ozone depletion. Current predictions are that the greenhouse effect will amount to between 1.5 and 4.5 degrees centigrade by the year 2030. This would mean that in temperate zones, winters might be wetter, and summers drier. The tropics would also become wetter, but the subtropics already dry, could become drier still. As the oceans warmed up and expanded, sea levels would rise, leading to severe flooding over low-level land.

The most obvious effect of climatic change will be on agriculture. A warmer climate is likely to move the areas for growing specific crops such as wheat, towards the poles. Marginal agriculture will suffer most because it will be unable to adapt easily to new conditions.

There will be widespread changes in natural ecosystems with grasslands and desert areas expanding, and forested areas shrinking and moving polewards. Problems such as desertification and soil erosion could worsen.

Ozone, a gas composed of three oxygen atoms, surrounds the earth like a delicate veil, protecting the planet and its inhabitants from the direct gaze of the sun. Were ozone not present in the atmosphere, lethal levels of ultraviolet radiation from the sun would reach the earth's surface.

Several chemicals used in or produced by industry greatly affect the speed at which ozone is broken down. These include the chlorofluorocarbons.

Changes of a few per cent in future ozone levels would be enough to let substantially more ultraviolet radition reach the earth's surface. Ultraviolet radiation is responsible for sunburn, snow blindness, eye damage, skin cancer and the ageing and wrinkling of the skin. It affects plant growth, slowing down photosynthesis and delaying germination of many plants, including trees and crops. Algae are particularly sensitive to ultraviolet radiation, raising fears that damage to the ozone layer could upset marine ecology and lower fish populations.

International action is urgently required to minimise both future greenhouse heating and ozone depletion. While something has already been done to control ozone depletion, little effort has gone into tackling the greenhouse problem which is, in many ways, the more serious issue.

There are four possible solutions to the greenhouse problem:

a. Reduce the rate at which fossil fuels are burnt and other greenhouse gases produced.

b. Dispose of the greenhouse gases as they are produced, elsewhere than in the atmosphere.

c. Recover the greenhouse gases already in the atmosphere and dispose of them elsewhere.

d. Accept the changing climate and adapt to it.

Only the first and the last solutions appear to be economically feasible. Carbon dioxide, for example, could be filtered from power station effluents, converted to some other chemical form and dumped on the ocean floor. But the cost would be enormous.

Carbon dioxide which is already in the atmosphere could, in theory, be 'mopped up' by planting more trees on the earth which would convert carbon dioxide into woody tissue. But an area the size of France would have to be planted annually to compensate for the current rate at which carbon dioxide is produced. Even if this were possible, the effects of the other greenhouse gases would still change future climate.

The most promising ways forward are to reduce the overall energy consumption, consume less fossil fuels by relying increasingly on nuclear and solar energy, for example, and learn to adapt and accept the changing climate. Future actions are likely to include a combination of these approaches, but international mechanisms to formulate an agreed plan have yet to be put into efffect.

(Source : *The Hindu*)

c. Answer the following questions.

   i. What probable climatic results will the greenhouse phenomenon have?

   ii. What are the efects of ozone depletion?

   iii. Which, according to the text, are economically feasible solutions to the greenhouse problem?

   What are the objections to the other solutions?

2. **Language focus** — 'The damage to the earth's atmosphere'

Fill in the blanks in the following passage with appropriate words. Compare your answer with your partner's.

I. Chemical pollution is changing the structure of the earth''s atmosphere, threatening to alter the climate and expose human populations to higher levels of dangerous ultra-violet .... The two major effects involved are the 'greenhouse effect' and damage to the .... layer .

The earth's atmosphere plays a crucial role in maintaining even .... on the earth's surface. Like the glass in a greenhouse, the atmosphere absorbs some of the long-wave radiation .... by the earth, and radiates energy back at the earth. If the atmosphere were not present, temperatures on the earth would be much .... than they are.

But .... activity is changing the atmosphere's structure. As .... like carbon dioxide are produced and released into the atmosphere, they absorb more of the earth's radition, and return more of it back to the earth.

The energy, which would otherwise escape harmlessly into space, is already increasing the earth's .... temperature, though so far by only small amounts (about 0.05°C) over the past 120 years.

.... is the most important of the greenhouse gases, and is produced primarily when............................ fuels are burnt to provide power. Levels of carbon dioxide in the atmosphere have already increased by some 25 per cent since the Industrial Revolution, they are expected to increase by a further 30 per cent in the next fifty years.

Many other gases also have a .... effect. These include nitrous oxide (laughing gas), methane, ozone and chlorofluorocarbons (CFCs, which are used in refrigeration and other industries). The .... of these gases in the atmosphere are much lower than that of carbon dioxide but they are increasing, and many of them produce a very strong greenhouse effect.

3. **Listening** — ' Noise pollution '

You are going to listen to a talk on noise pollution. Listen carefully and write your notes in the chart below:

Study conducted in	Findings

4. **Writing** — 'Noise pollution'

a. Discuss with your partner some measures to check noise pollution in metropolitan areas.

b. Write a set of recommendations to check noise pollution.

Follow-up

1. **Comprehension check**

   Look back at the text, 'Cleaning the Cooum' on pages 108 -110, and answer the following questions.

   a. Which of the following statements best expresses the main idea of the text?

      i. The text shows how a spirited American woman got the river cleaned.

      ii. The text describes the river and shows how it gets polluted.

      iii. The text describes the health hazards resulting from the pollution of the river.

   b. Thiagarajan's main concern was to

      i. raise money for the river-cleaning project;

      ii. show how the American approach could be effective when other approaches have failed.

      iii. to make the citizens aware of their responsibilities.

   c. What, according to Thiagarajan, is the reason for the failure of schemes of improvement?

d. What, according to the text, is the American government's approach to issues which it has failed to solve?

e. Complete the following sentences using the information given in the passage.

   i. The river mouth can be kept open by removing the sand bar when it forms, but ....

   ii. Sea water can be used to flush out the stagnant water, but ....

   iii. Western technologies may be effective, but ....

2. **Oral practice**

Hold a conversation on the problem of noise pollution in cities.

Student A: You are a citizen affected by noise pollution from various sources. Express your feelings strongly and demand corrective measures.

Student B : You are a police official. You appreciate the citizen's feelings and would like to be helpful. But you have practical difficulties in enforcing regulations.

Student C: You are a bus driver. You do not like using the horn unnecessarily. But you cannot help it when people have no road sense.

Before you start the conversation, spend five minutes preparing what you will say. Make use of the text, 'Noise pollution in Madras', on pages 112-113 if necessary.

3. **Writing skills development**

You happen to live in an area where political meetings are held frequently as a matter of practice. There is no check on the use of loudspeakers at these meetings. Write a letter to the editor of a newspaper complaining about the situation.

4. Language check

Look at the following sentences and punctuate them. Check by looking back at lines 48-53 of the text on page 109.

> deborah thiagarajan has immense faith in the redeeming power of human involvement when the citizens for clean waterways initiated by intach in madras launched its drive to collect one million signatures with a minimum voluntary donation of one rupee per person it was an exercise she says in identifying one million people who care

Environment Unit 2

Ecology versus development

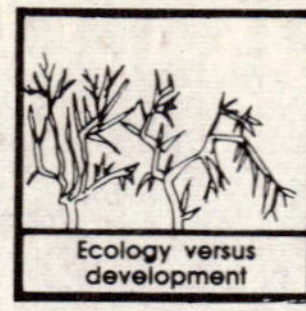

Preparation

1. Language development

a. You are already familiar with some prefixes and suffixes. Here are a few more which will figure in the texts of this Unit.

Prefixes:

'con-' has the meaning of 'with' as in 'conjunction'.

'amphi-' has the meaning of 'both' as in 'amphitheatre'.

'sub-' has the meaning of 'under' as in 'submerge'.

'ad-' has the meaning of 'intensification' as in 'adduce'.

Suffixes which make nouns from verbs :

'-ence', -ment', and '-ing'

Give examples of words with each of the prefixes and suffixes mentioned above. Write sentences using them.

b. Match the words in column A with their meanings in column B. Make sure you can pronounce all the words in column A correctly.

	A		B
i.	conservation	a.	organism able to live both on land and in water
ii.	genetic	b.	biology dealing with mutual relations between organisms and their environment
iii.	amphibian	c.	reservoir, a place where water is collected and stored
iv.	submergence	d.	preservation

v.	ecology	e.	a reciprocal action or effect
vi.	afforestation	f.	pertaining to plant and animal breeding
vii.	deforestation	g.	expansion of forests
viii.	catchment	h.	being placed under water
ix.	repercussion	i.	cutting down
x.	felling	j.	clearing of forests

c. *Fill in the blank spaces in the box given below with the appropriate form of the word.*

noun	adjective	person concerned
environment	________	________
nature	________	________
________	ecological	________
________	________	conservationist
________	________	geneticist

d. *Look at the following examples and fill in the chart below.*

	present	past	past participle
a.	fall	fell	fallen
b.	fell	felled	felled
a.	see	______	______
b.	______	______	______
a.	find	______	______
b.	______	______	______

Produce three sentences with the three words in (b) in any form.

2. Oral practice

Discuss the following in small groups.

a. What do you understand by the expression 'environmental conservation'? Specify three ways in which environment can be preserved.

b. Do you think that environmental conservation acts as a brake on economic development?

c. What is meant by environmental degradation? Specify three ways in which the environment is degraded.

d. Do you agree that environmental degradation leads to social injustices?

Be ready to report to the class when the teacher asks you to.

3. Writing skills development

Write a paragraph describing how the environment can be preserved.

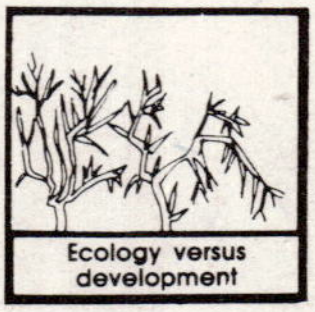

Part 1

1. Reading — 'Paper mills and destruction of bamboo forests'

a. i. Look at the title of the following text. Write down 10-15 words which you expect to find in the passage. Compare your list with your neighbour's.

ii. Talk to another student and list three or four things the passage is likely to include.

iii. Now read the passage and check whether the words you chose in (i) appeared or not. Which words might have appeared but did not?

iv. Did the passage deal with any of the points you listed? Do you think that the passage did not deal with something it ought to have dealt with?

Paper Mills and Destruction of Bamboo Forests

Bamboos have been used by human beings since time immemorial. But it is only in the last four to five decades that industries have come to recognise their value. Owing to the installation of paper mills in India, in particular, bamboo became a valuable resource. Today, it is heavily exploited with the result that large bamboo forests have already disappeared.

Ecology versus development

The development of paper mills in Karnataka and Tamil Nadu is playing havoc with the bamboo forests of these states and increasingly with the bamboo resources of other states as local bamboo forests get depleted. Bamboo today forms about 67 per cent of the raw material used by paper mills, which continue to expand. Since demand is far outstripping supply, the pressure on extracting bamboo is becoming intense.

The disappearance of bamboo stocks is having major environmental repercussions. Bamboo is a very good soil binder. The reduction in bamboo stocks inevitably brings about increased soil erosion. Ecologically, bamboo is a sun-loving species which can grow profusely, wherever the canopy of moist or dry deciduous forest is opened up. With the disappearance of bamboo this ecological niche is being taken over rapidly by a weed called 'Eupatorium glandulosum', particularly in the moister tracts. Once this weed takes over, it smothers and totally suppresses all other regeneration. It dries up in the dry-season and promotes intense forest fires. Eupatorium is neither a good soil binder nor a soil builder like the bamboo. No animal touches it and its spread leads to a serious loss of even grazing lands.

The overexploitation of bamboo stocks by the paper mills has had its adverse impact on the life of human beings too. Thousands of poor villagers have suffered greatly because of this. They depend on bamboo for food, house construction, manufacture of agricultural implements such as seed drills, and for making mats and baskets, an important source of livelihood. For them bamboo is a means of survival.

Just about 15 years ago, the basket weavers of Kampanaickanpalayam, a village near the town of Sathyamangalam in Tamil Nadu,used to go into neighbouring forests, spend about half a day collecting bamboo and then come back and start weaving. The old and others who could not go themselves used to pay Rs 6 per headload of bamboo. An average family would earn about Rs 8 per day. There was also an uninterrupted supply of the right quantity and quality of bamboo.

Today, with the Seshasayee Paper Mill as a major competitor for the same resource, bamboo supply has become a major problem for the poor. Now some villagers specialise in collecting bamboo illegally and selling it to the weavers. These people have to travel nearly 25 miles to collect enough bamboo and it takes about three days. Each headload now costs anything above Rs 30; consequently, even with prices of bamboo goods having risen, the weavers earn less than before. Moreover, the bamboo supply is no longer assured. Whenever the forest officials catch the bamboo collectors, the supply is cut off for weeks.

This situation, which is obviously leading to much resentment, calls for a humanistic approach on the part of the government authorities concerned.

(Source: *The State of India's Environment : 1982*)

b. *Answer the following questions:*

i. What evidence is there in the text for assuming the following?

   a. Plenty of bamboo of good variety was available in the past.
   b. Not everyone had to go to the forest to collect bamboo.
   c. The destruction of bamboo is creating a problem for the cattle.
   d. The destruction of bamboo stocks in one place affects the stocks in other places, too.

ii. Note down all the words and phrases in the passage which refer to the destruction of bamboo.

2. **Language focus** — 'Dams'

Some of the words in the box belong to the text which follows. Read the text carefully once, then try to fill in the gaps with the most appropriate word.

distribute	proliferate	exploitation	depend
catchment	economic	aquatic	urban
problem	conviction	defend	among
triggering	ecological	eviction	disturb

Dams and their Adverse Environmental Effects

Big dams have had several adverse effects on the environment and the people. Some of them are: the .... of thousands of families and their resettlement at some other site, making them refugees in their own land; the increase in the incidence of some diseases; .... of earthquakes and dam bursts; and the destruction of ecosystems. The last mentioned consequence has been a cause for great concern .... people.

The design and constructions of dams in India have been achieved mainly as civil engineering tasks neglecting their harmful .... impact. Engineers seem to be concerned with instant solutions of problems rather than the long-term effects and consequences of the solutions proposed. Thus, the provision of the intended benefits to downstream areas causes the neglect or wanton .... of the environment of the catchment regions upstream in most cases. Its immediate victims are the tribals the peasants in the river valleys and the hillfolk whose lives.... .... on the resources provided by their immediate environment. This is, of course, a pitiable situation. But more so is the ecological ruin with its grave long-range .... consequences for the nation.

The decimation of vital forests in the .. .. areas is one of the most serious problems effected by the engineering approach. Large tracts of forests have been lost as a result, particularly in the Himalayan hills and the western

Ghats. Submerging forest lands have aggravated the ....

Large scale deforestation for dams can lead to subtle imbalances in the ecosystem. Following the construction of dams, ... life is often grievously harmed. Changes in water velocity, water chemistry, temperature and turbidity .... the free pasage of fish to and from their spawning grounds. Weeds often .... in irrigation reservoirs. The spread of diseases among human beings and cattle is often due to many of these weeds.

(Source : *The State of India's Environment, 1982*)

Check your answers with your neighbour.

3. **Discussion** — 'A matter of survival'

Here is an excerpt from a report on theWorld Forestry Congress held in Jakarta in 1978. Read it and discuss in groups how forest resources will be able to provide humanity with all those things mentioned in the report. Be ready to report your views to the class when the teacher asks you to.

> The Congress appealed to the people of all nations and their governments to recognise the importance of forest resources for the biosphere and the survival of humanity and to devote themselves to safeguarding and promoting these resources which will provide humanity with food, raw materials, energy, rural wellbeing, ecological protection and improvement in the quality of life.

4. **Writing** — 'The importance of forest resources'

Write a paragraph on the measures you would recommend to preserve forest resources.

Ecology versus development

Part 2

1. **Reading — 'Silent Valley'**

   a. Discuss the following in groups.

      i. Have you heard of Silent Valley?

      ii. Do you know where it is located?

      iii. In what connection did it become prominent?

      iv. What is the present status of Silent Valley?

   b. Now read the following passage on 'Silent Valley'. As you read it make brief notes on the lines suggested below.

      a. Silent Valley — its location ....
      its richness ....
      the river flowing through it ....

      b. The flora and fauna of the valley — i ....
      ii ....
      iii ....

      c. The Kerala Government — its proposal ....
      the rationale behind the proposal i ....
      ii ....
      iii ....

      d. Campaign — against what?..
      the reasons for it i ....
      ii ....
      iii ....

      the nature of it ....

      e. the fate of the project..

Silent Valley : A case study in the environment versus development debate

Silent Valley is a tropical rain forest area at the southern end of the Western Ghats in the Malabar region of Kerala. It is one of the richest biological and genetic heritages in the world. It recently shot into prominence when the government of Kerala proposed a hydroelectric project on its site. The proposal envisaged the generation of hydro-power by damming the Kuntipuzha river flowing through this valley. A drop of 857 metres, the highest in the state, makes it an ideal site for a hydel project. Malabar is one of the least developed areas of Kerala. The per capita consumption of electrical energy in this region is only a quarter of the state-wide figure. It was also felt that the project will have immense potential for employment.

But there was an instant campaign against the project as it posed a threat of extinction to the tremendous variety of biological species that have evolved over hundreds of millions of years. The campaign brought together a remarkable number of individuals and organisations. The list of organisations includes among others, the Kerala Sastra Sahitya Parishad, the National Committee on Environmental Planning, the Bombay Natural History Society, World Wildlife Fund (India), Friends of Trees, the International Union for Conservation of Nature, and the press. The Central Government requested the state of Kerala to abandon the project, too.

It was estimated that the project, if and when completed, would make only a marginal contribution to the power position in the state — a mere seven per cent of the total demand for electricity in Kerala by 1990-91. This would certainly not be worth the ecological damage that the project would cause.

'Even a preliminary study of the peripheral areas of the valley has yielded information on over 900 species of flowering plants and ferns.Several specimens that have become extinct elsewhere are found in the Silent Valley', says the Botanical Survey of India. A few plants collected by it are new to science. The vegetation abounds in medicinal and aromatic plants as also wild relatives of spice and pulse yielding plants. The latter have shown an enormous amount of genetic diversity with respect to disease resistance and protein content.

The Zoological Survey of India has identified several rare and endangered faunal species including butterflies, birds, fish, amphibians, reptiles and mammals in the Silent Valley. Three amphibian species were previously unknown. Many insects and birds like the black-orange flycatcher, the white-browed bulbul, the hill myna and the hornbills are endemic to this area. Three endangered mammals, the lion-tailed macaque, the tiger and the Wilgiri tahr are also found here. The lion-tailed macaque is one of the most endangered mammals in the world.

Going ahead with the hydel project would have resulted in the loss of this precious treasure referred to above. The campaigners against the project could convincingly make out the case that the needs of the people of Malabar for energy, irrigation and employment could be safely met in other ways. In this way the campaign has been successful in saving Silent Valley from submergence resulting from an irrigation and hydel project. This indicates the stand that development, however desirable, should not be at the cost of environment.

(Source : *The State of India's Environment*, 1982)

2. **Writing** — 'Development at the cost of environment?'

Do you agree that development should not be at the cost of environment? Write a paragraph expressing your views on the question.

3. **Listening** — 'The environmental movement in India'

You are going to listen to a talk about the environmental movement in India. Listen carefully for the details and take notes of as many of them as you can on the lines indicated below.

a. Government measures and schemes ....

....

....

....

b. Voluntary efforts ....

....

c. Aim of the environmental movement ....

....

4. **Role play** — 'The Chipko movement

Student A : You are a journalist. You want to write an article about the Chipko movement. You are going to interview M M Sunderlal Bahuguna, one of the leaders of the movement. Prepare a list of questions to ask him.

Student B : You are Mr Sundarlal Bahuguna, one of the leaders of the Chipko movement. You are going to be interviewed by a journalist who will ask you questions about the movement. Prepare yourself to answer them.

Make use of the notes taken on the environmental movement in India to frame the questions as well as to answer them. Start when you are both ready.

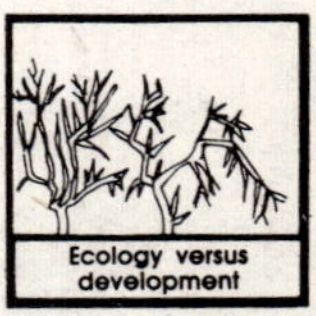

Follow-up

1. **Comprehension check**

Look back at the passage on Silent Valley and say whether the following statements are true or false. Correct the false ones.

14

a. When the Silent Valley project was proposed, people immediately protested against it.

b. The lion-tailed macaque is the most dangerous mammal in the world.

c. Silent Valley was submerged by an irrigation and hydel project.

d. From the point of view of generation of electricity, Silent Valley is an excellently suitable place.

2. **Writing skills development**

Using the notes taken by you in the listening exercise on pages 167 and 168, write a paragraph on the measures taken by the government for environmental conservation.

3. **Oral practice**

Work in pairs. Using the notes made by you on Silent Valley on page 129, ask and answer questions about Silent Valley. Use question words such as *where, what, which, why, how*, etc. Try to answer the questions as quickly and clearly as you can.

4. **Language development**

The terms *cause* and *effect* refer to the relation between events, occurrences, etc. The cause of an event is the reason for it. The event is itself the effect or the result of the cause.

e.g. Scarcity is the cause of the rise in price of articles.

The verbal forms of 'cause' and 'result' can also be used to express the same relation.

e.g. The rise in price of articles is caused by scarcity.

Now look for at least ten words or phrases in the texts of this unit expressing causal relations. Check with your neighbour. If you have time look for five more. Now your teacher will check with the class.

Environment Unit 3

Our living environment

Preparation

1. Language development

Read the following newspaper report.

Bhubaneswar, Aug 11.

The Forest Department officials of the Orissa Government are unable to decide on what to do with an elephant which has won their hearts each time they tried to capture it. Last year, they attempted to tranquillise it but when they were ready to fire the dart, the elephant raised its trunk and saluted them, and that convinced the officials that it was not a wild elephant. But now they are in the soup. This year, the elephant has been sighted again, but with a difference. It is now moving about with a girlfriend.

Last year, two persons were killed by the tusker in Paikmal area in Sambalpur District, following which the people of the area petitioned the Government to take action. The Forest Department officials decided to capture the elephant and bring it to the Nandan Kanan Zoo at Bhubaneswar. They waited for ten days to capture the elephant but in vain.

One of the officials who came face to face with the elephant, was all set to fire the tranquillising dart but stopped as soon as he noticed the elephant raising its trunk and saluting him, pleading not to shoot. The elephant then disappeared into the forest.

The officials were unable to decide what line of action to take when the elephant reappeared near Bolingur town and injured an old woman. Surprisingly, the elphant has now come out of the forest with a girlfriend and is moving about freely scaring the villagers.

According to the officials, the elephant was left fending for itself by its mahout about seven years back. The elephant had gone into the forests, but has now returned, perhaps because it was not accepted by elephant herds. Though the elephant was not termed wild, it was hurting people coming in its way.

(Source : The Hindu)

Using the information given in the report, match the cause with the effect in the two sets of sentences given below.

Cause

The elephant herds did not accept it.

The elephant was accompanied by a girlfriend.

The elephant killed two persons.

The mahout deserted him.

The elephant raised its trunk and saluted them.

Result

The officials could not decide on what to do with the elephant.

The officials did not shoot the tranquillising dart.

The elephant returned to the village.

The people of Paikmal petitioned the government.

The elephant went into the forests.

Now link the cause and effect using connecting words like *because, since* and *as*. After you have written the sentences, rewrite them using *therefore, consequently* and *as a result* : note that with these three connectives, you get two separate sentences, or two main clauses connected by *and*.

2. **Reading skills development**

Read the following text and answer the questions.

A. Salim Ali was one of the most restless of men and the story of his extraordinarily long life spent mostly in the open constitutes a glorious chapter in the history of world ornithology. The pioneer Indian ornithologist and environmentalist has made a sterling contribution to the field of ornithology. His life was avidly dedicated to the study of birds in their natural habitat.

B. His work of over fifty years has been instrumental in the protection of bird life, the setting up of parks and reserves. His message has gone high and low across the land and we are sure that weaver birds weave his initials in their nests and swifts perform parabolas in the sky in his honour.

C. In his autobiography, *Fall of a Sparrow*, he recaptures instances when he and his nephew as little children used to buy partridges and quails from markets with the intention of setting them free. He also recalls hearing the spirited song of the magpie robin in the morning as one of his cherished ornithological memories.

D. Salim Ali was not only a great naturalist but an explorer. He knew every square inch of India, and travelled more extensively in the country than some of the eminent freedom fighters including Mahatma Gandhi and Nehru. The very volume of his field work and the precision of it earn him a place among the great naturalists of the

world. As a young boy he made a number of sparrow-hunting expeditions and in his opinion, 'the scientific interest in birds' is a 'fortuitous offshoot' of these expeditions.

E. Even though he considered birds his passionate friends, as an ornithologist his love for them was never of the sentimental type. For a scientific approach to bird study, it was often necessary for him to sacrifice a few of his treasured birds, and while mentioning this killing of birds in his autobiography, he affirms, 'I do not enjoy the killing, and sometimes even suffer a prick of the conscience .... alas ...... it would have been impossible to advance our taxonomical knowledge of Indian birds but for the methodical collection of specimens'.

F. Meticulous observation and verification of data, journeying through forest and desert unmindful of hazards: such was his work for a lifetime ....There are more than 2000 species of birds in India and they form a natural blessing perhaps unmatched by that of any other country. Salim Ali has studied quite a few of these birds and written scientific descriptions of them. He has written a number of books including the monumental ten-volume *Handbook of the Birds of India and Pakistan* (in collaboration with Dillon Ripley)... His autobiography is a very lively work, notable for its wit and humour. His wife, Tehmina, emerges as a great lady in this work: she was ready to make sacrifices to enable her husband to pursue his work.

G. While living in Dehra Dun in 1934 he attempted to do research on economic ornithology, which includes detailed studies on the food and feeding habits of birds. In his opinion, birds on the one hand can be highly destructive to cereal crops and orchard fruits: on the other hand 'they can be highly beneficial in controlling the ravages of insects, pests and other vermin such as rodents'. He also championed their cause by saying that they effect cross pollination and 'are thus of great usefulness in the propagation of plants'. Another area which always fascinated him is the problem of camouflaging colouration of desert animals and birds. After a thorough study, he concluded that the greater exposure to ultraviolet radiation results in greater paleness of colour and attributed to this cause the sandy colour of desert birds and animals.

H. He was totally, relentlessly immersed in his work. He was interested in that kind of work which is its own reward. It is the 'scientific temper' of Salim Ali that the young generation must try to understand. This kind of scientifc temper is not learned through a mere reading of physics or chemistry. It is a method, a discipline. There is no room for the merely glamorous. The scientific temper goes hand in hand with sustained, unruffled, silent work.

I. Now that Salim Ali is no more, who will speak about ecology and conservation with passion and fearlessness? Ornithology will receive a spurt only if people take greater interest in nature. Even the so-called scientific temper is born of one's interest in nature. If this interest is lacking in the younger generation, is our education system to be blamed or is something else to be blamed?

a. Read paragraph B again. What does the author say about weaver birds and swifts? Are these statements true?

b. Compare what is said in paragraph C and paragraph E. How do you explain the difference in Salim Ali's treatment of birds on these two occasions?

c. Why is it necessary to collect data on birds and describe birds?

d. In what ways are birds useful to man? In what ways are they harmful to man?

e. What do you know about camouflage among animals and among birds? Can you give an example from your everyday experience?

f. Is camouflage always a conscious attempt on the part of animals to escape from enemies? Discuss Salim Ali's findings about desert animals.

g. Can you say what the scientific temper is, and what it is not?

3. **Writing skills development**

Write brief descriptions of an animal and a bird familiar to you. Here are some hints to describe a cat.

smaller than a dog – mammal – quadruped (having four legs) – many colours – furry skin – soft paws – eyes can adapt to darkness – carnivorous – kills and eats rats and other little animals – good as pet

After you write your descriptions, compare them with your neighbour's.

4. **Oral practice**

People hold different opinions about the following subjects. After a discussion in groups, speak in support of either side of the argument. One student from each side of the argument can speak. Others can ask questions.

i. The use of animals for scientific experiments

ii. Eating non-vegetarian food

iii. Export of ivory, snake-skins and crocodile skins from India.

Part 1

1. **Listening** — 'Animals and plants'

We know that animals differ from plants, but how do they differ from each other? You will now hear a talk on 'Animals and Plants'. Listen for the points of difference and complete the table given below.

features	animals	plants	exceptions

2. **Discussion** — 'Bird study'

In the preceding pages, you read about Ṣalim Ali, the distinguished Indian ornithologist. Bird study is a very interesting pursuit. Here is a list of aids which can be used for the study of birds:

binoculars
camera with telescopic lens
movie camera
tape recorder

microphone
rings to be attached to the bird's leg

Can you think of any other aids? Here are some aspects of bird life which you can study:

daily cycle of a bird's life (rising early or late, when active and when inactive, etc)
food habits
feeding young ones
birdsong and communication among birds
social behaviour of birds (territorial defence, courtship, nesting)

Discuss in small groups how different methods can be used to study these aspects of bird life. After the discussion one member of the group can tell the class about the aspect studied and the method adopted. Here is an example:

" We can use binoculars to observe birds from a distance. If we go near the birds they may get scared and fly away. If they are with their young ones, they may attack us. One aspect of their life we can observe is........ (*Continue the answer.*)

3. **Reading** — 'An interview with an ornithologist'

One of the landmarks in the history of bird study in India is the monumental ten-volume *Handbook of the Birds of India and Pakistan* which Salim Ali wrote in collaboration with Dr Dillon Ripley. Padma Bhushan Dillon Ripley delivered the first Salim Ali Memorial Lecture in March 1988. Here are excerpts from an interview with him by Rashmi Sehgal.

Dr Ripley, you have devoted a lifetime to the study of birds. At what age did you get interested in them?

Dillon Ripley : Well, I really don't remember. I must have been interested in them from a very early age. I always liked nature and being out of doors. My mother was curious about why I seemed to like birds a lot, although she liked birds herself. Everybody in the family was very sympathetic to nature and the outdoors. I must have had a special feeling. I think part of it stemmed from the fact that I had a very, very good eyesight; so I trained myself early to see things. When I started to drive a car at 16, I would be driving with someone in the family and I would say, 'Look at that bird.' And they would say, 'Hey! How on earth did you manage to spot that bird while you were driving! I realised that I was perhaps more observant than others. It was gradual, training myself to spot objects and looking for colour.

Of course, birds are like human beings, have a very acute and well-developed colour sense. That's what birds' lives are all about; because, for catching prey, eating it, establishment of mating and nesting and so on, colour is everything. That is not so with the majority of the mammals. We humans are one of the few mammals that have a well-defined colour sense. Dogs, for example, are colour bind. They see in shades of grey and brown. Certain other animals have a good colour sense, certain fish and some of the reptiles, but we are just lucky. It means so much to us. You only realise how important it is when you are colour blind.

How did you first happen to visit India?

It happened because of a very fortuitous circumstance. A close friend of my sister was getting married to someone from outside our town. He had been offered a job as head of the hostel in the University of Nagpur. The bride's family requested us to put him up with us because we had a large house. He came to stay with us. One night, we were all sitting around a fire, and he said 'We would love it if you could come and see us in India,' and my mother asked us,' What do you think? Would you like to do that, children?' We all said we would love to. My brothers and sisters, who were eight or ten years older than I, had just finished their education and I was beginning my high school. So she approached the headmaster of my school. He was quite considerate and gave me a year's leave. We all set sail in different ways. My brothers and sisters, who set sail earlier, came via Japan and China. My mother and I came a little later through Egypt on the Peninsular and Orient Line and we landed in Bombay. Later, we joined them in Calcutta.

That was the beginning of the long association you have had with India?

Yes. It started in 1927. I came back in the 1930s and in the 1940s when I served in the war, mostly in Ceylon. It was then that I made my acquaintance with Salim Ali in Bombay, and we became very good friends right away. We made a list of all the places we could explore together that had been overlooked by the British, for one reason or another, in terms of the fauna, such as the hills of what is now called Arunachal Pradesh, Orissa, parts of the south and parts of the east coast. You know, there are some parts of the Eastern Ghats, north of Madras and south of Seringapatam, that have not been studied to this day. So you'll see I'll soon be back.

After you drew up the list,Dr Ripley, when did you actually begin to visit these places?

Almost every year or every other year. As Salim and I travelled from one place to another, we found we were falling into a pattern,because, by a coincidence, we just happened to visit these particular places 25 years after someone else had been there. And that revealed the great changes that had taken place in the environment over the years.

Changes like — ?

For example, in the 1930s, a survey had been made of the bird species and fauna in a particular area of the Deccan. When we reached the area we found many of the species missing. We began to examine why this had happened. One of the things we found responsible for this was the policy of developing reserved forests, which the British had worked very hard at. Maintaining these reserved forests of teak and sal by cleaning up the understory , the bush, made the forest look very beautiful and immaculate, but it began to show a decline in the species of birds. The British had created an artificial environment instead of a natural environment.

This is something that foresters have not realised even today, with their emphasis on eucalyptus plantations and so on.

Yes. It is terribly destructive. It's a slow death. All these monocultures that are being encouraged are very destructive in the long run. Foresters don't realise it because the period is too long. By the time the problem surfaces, they will have retired from their jobs. Whatever they do may seem useful economically but it is bad science.

Another aspect I would like to stress is that although there is a much greater variety of species to be found in the tropical regions, the number of each species is much smaller. So, if their environment is destroyed, the chances of a particular species becoming extinct are that much greater. In the temperate regions, the varieties are far fewer, but their numbers are much larger, helping to ensure that a species is never wiped out completely.

One of your– and of course Salim Ali's – most enduring contributions to the field of ornithology is the ten-volume magnum opus on the birds of the subcontinent on which both of you collaborated. Were there any problems that you and Salim Ali faced while writing the book?

Our main problem was one of distance. I was in America, he was in India, and so it took a long time to get our points across. Luckily, he had a couple of assistants and I also had one. There was a tremendous amount of correspondence, correcting little things that couldn't be allowed to pass, and also a great deal of editorial work. We had some people from the Oxford University Press working on it full time, because it was a massive project, filling ten volumes. There were an infinite variety of species that we had to reckon with. We had to check all the names and everything else to avoid mistakes that were constantly creeping in, especially in the names. Someone had used one name, someone else had used another name, and how were we to determine which was the right name? It took an awful lot of time and effort.

The actual field work didn't take too much time?

That was the shortest and most fun part of the whole thing because when you do field work you are out in the open, living in tents or little dak bungalows and you are having a great time. Sometimes when it starts raining or the local people turn hostile or the jeep breaks down, it's different — but that's rare.

(Source : *Span*)

Answer the following questions on the text.

a. What, according to Ripley, is the faculty that seemed most important to him as a boy for bird study?

b. Different animals have different degrees of vision. What does the text say about this with reference to man, other mammals, birds, dogs, fish and reptiles?

c. Why does Ripley say that his visit to India was fortuitous?

d. What did Ripley and Salim Ali do in the early days of their association?

e. What was the 'pattern' that they discovered in their work? What could they learn from this pattern?

f. How did the figures in the 1930 survey turn out to be wrong?

g. What was the aim of the British in developing reserved forests? Do you think that they were aware of the long-term consequences of the policy? What were these consequences?

h. Why is it that foresters do not realise the harm done by their programmes of forest development?

i. Why are the tropical species of birds in greater danger than the species of the temperate regions?

j. Which parts of the interview would you consider to be of

interest to the general reader, and which parts to be of interest to the environment planner? Why? Can you think of any important recommendation that an environment planner could make after reading the interview?

4. **Language focus**—'The compensation'

Read the following story carefully, and note what happens in it.

Paterson was a businessman. He once bought a new car. He was fond of driving and spent a lot of time driving the car along the streets of his town. Later he drove into the countryside.

One day he was driving along a road on the edge of a forest. On one side was a beautiful river, and on the other side was the forest. In the distance he could see a small village.

The scenery was so beautiful that Paterson could not take his eyes off it. 'I should spend my next vacation in that village. I should bring my wife and children with me,' he said to himself

All on a sudden he saw a man in front of his car. The man was leading a dog by a leash.

He tried to stop the car, but it was too late. The man jumped aside; but the car ran over the dog, which died on the spot.

Paterson got out of the car and said to the man, 'I'm very sorry. It was my mistake. I didn't see you, as I was lost in the beauty of the place.... And the dog? Is it yours?'

The man said, 'Yes, it's mine.'

'I am sorry that I have killed your dog. I don't know how I can make amends.'

Paterson took his briefcase and gave the man some money. 'I hope you will accept it. The dog is dead and there's nothing we can do about it. Please accept it.'

The man took the money and put it in his pocket.

Paterson turned to get into his car. It was then that noticed the gun which the man was carrying.

'I see you were going hunting,' said Paterson. 'I am so sorry I spoiled your fun.'

'Oh, no,' said the man. 'I was not going hunting. This dog has been very ill for three weeks now, and has been suffering terrible pain. I could not bear to see his suffering, and wanted to put an end to his pain. So I was taking him to the forest to shoot him. But now that won't be necessary, since he is dead. Anyway, thank you for the money.'

Imagine that you meet the man who got the money from Paterson. He tells you his story. Given below is the story as told by the man. Supply the appropriate forms of the verbs given in brackets:

'One day I was (walk) along the road leading to the village with my dog when all on a sudden a car (appear) before me. The man at the wheel (drive) the car very fast. I (see) the car just in time and (jump) to a side. But the dog (run over) by the car and died.

The man (stop) the car and (come) to me. He (say) that he (not see) me because he had been lost in admiration of the scenery.

He (take) out his briefcase and (give) me some money. He (say) that the dog was dead and there (be) nothing we (can) do about it. I (take) the money.

Then the man (see) the gun I (carry). He (say) that he (be)sorry to have spoiled my hunting. Obviously, he (think) that I was going hunting because I (have) the dog and the gun with me.

I (tell) him that I (not go) hunting. I (explain) that the dog (be) ill for three weeks. It (suffer) great pain. So I (want) to end his suffering and (take) him to the forest to shoot him. But now that (be) not necessary because the dog (be) dead. I (thank) the man for the money and (bid) him goodbye.

Our living environment

Part 2

1. **Listening** —'The forests of India'

Listen to the talk on the different types of forests of India. As you listen, write down the details in the table below.

type of forest	altitude; climate	names of trees	uses of trees

2. **Reading** — 'Vanishing animals'

The following text is from the writings of Gerald Durrell, who loved animals, cared for them and strove to save those animals which were in danger. Read the text and answer the questions.

> Unfortunately, the Pere David deer and the white-tailed gnu are not the only creatures in the world that are nearly extinct...
>
> *From this sentence, can you guess what the author has said in the preceding paragraphs? What do you expect the author to say in the remaining part of the text?*

The list of creatures that have vanished altogether, and others that have almost vanished, is a long and melancholy one. As man has spread across the earth he has wrought the most terrible havoc among the wild life by shooting, trapping, cutting and burning the forest, and by the callous and stupid introduction of enemies where there were no enemies before.

Take the dodo, for example, the great ponderous wedding pigeon, the size of a goose, that inhabited the island of Mauritius. Secure in its island home, this bird had lost the power of flight since there were no enemies to fly from, and , since there were no enemies, it nested on the ground in complete safety. But, as well as losing the power of flight, it seems to have lost the power of recognising an enemy when it saw one, for apparently it was an extremely tame and confiding creature. Then...

Before you read on, look at the word, 'Then ....' What do you expect the author to say next?

Then man discovered the dodos' paradise in about 1507, and with him came his evil familiars: dogs, cats, pigs, rats and goats. The dodo surveyed these new arrivals with an air of innocent interest. Then the slaughter began. The goats ate the undergrowth which provided the dodo with cover; dogs and cats hunted and harried the old birds: while pigs grunted their way round the island, eating the eggs and young and rats followed behind to finish the feast. By 1681 the fat ungainly and harmless pigeon was extinct — as dead as the dodo.

All over the world the wild fauna has been whittled down steadily and remorselessly, and many lovely and interesting animals have been so reduced in numbers that, without protection and help, they can never re-establish themselves. If they cannot find sanctuary where they can live and breed undisturbed, their numbers will dwindle until they join the dodo, the quagga and the great auk on the long list of extinct creatures.

Of course, in the last decade or so, much has been done for the protection of wild life: sanctuaries and reserves have been started, and the reintroduction of a species into areas where it had become extinct is taking place. In Canada, for instance, beavers are now reintroduced into certain areas by means of aeroplane. The animal is put in a special box attached to a parachute, and when the plane flies over the area it drops the cage and its beaver passenger out. The cage floats down on the end of the parachute and when it hits the ground it opens automatically and the beaver then makes its way to the nearest stream or lake.

But although much is being done, there is still a very great deal to do. Unfortunately, the majority of useful work in animal preservation has been done mainly for animals which are of some economic importance to man and there are many obscure species of no economic importance which, although they are protected on paper, as it were, are in actual fact being allowed to die out because nobody, except a few interested zoologists, considers them important enough to spend money on.

a. Man is responsible for the destruction of animal species, both directly and indirectly. What does the text say about his direct responsibility? In some cases man did not himself destroy the animals, he introduced certain other factors that led to the destruction of animals. What were these factors?

b. What evidence is there in the text to show that an animal may lose a faculty if it does not make use of it?

c. Pick out the adjectives in the text that show the sadness, the cruelty and the foolishness of the destruction of animals.

d. What are the efforts being made at present to preserve wildlife?

Learner awareness

The text you have just read contains a large number of new words. Still, you were able to understand the points the author wanted to make. For understanding a text, it is not necessary to know all the words in it. The meanings of many words can be guessed from the context. Don't be put off by unfamiliar words in what you are reading.

e. After reading the last paragraph, decide which of the following sentences sums up the author's attitude.

   i. Animals must be preserved because they are useful to man.

   ii. Animals must be preserved because animal life is pre cious.

   iii. Animals must be preserved because animals are weak and affectionate.

   iv. Animals must be preserved because they are dumb creatures.

   v. None of the above.

2. **Role play** — 'Animals as pets'

Student A : You and Student B live next door to each other. B is fond of dogs and has an Alsatian as a pet. You want to tell B that it is not good to have pets in the house. Think of the points you can make.

Student B : You are fond of animals and have a pet dog in your house. When Student A tells you that it is not good to have pets around, you want to convince him that there are many advantages in keeping a pet dog at home. Prepare yourself for the role.

Begin when both of you are ready.

4. **Language focus** — 'Animals and plants'

Look at the following sentences.

> Animals can communicate with each other. Plants cannot communicate with each other.

In the second sentence the predicate of the first sentence is repeated, with the addition of 'not'. It is possible to use a short form of the predicate, avoiding the repetition:

> Animals can communicate with each other, but plants can't.

Read the following sentences and add a contracted form of the predicate, as in the above example:

a. An animal is able to move about freely, but a plant...

b. The size and shape of an animal are fixed, but those...

c. Plants manufacture their own food, but ...

d. The structure of a plant cell is rigid, but ...

e. A plant cell contains cellulose, but...

f. In winter an animal or a bird will move to a warm place, but...

g. Animals take care of their offspring, but...

h. Plants use sunlight to manufacture food, but...

In the above sentences, we have stated the differences between animals and plants. Look at the following sentence in which a similarity is expressed using a shortened form of the predicate.

> A plant uses food as a source of energy. So does an animal.

Read the following sentences. and then add a second sentence expressing the idea of similarity.

i. A plant can digest complex foods. So ...

j. An animal can transport food within its body ...

k. Animals require water for normal life...

l. Animals produce hormones within the body ...

m. Animals are sensitive to the environment ...

n. Animals can reproduce themselves ...

Follow-up

1. Comprehension check

Look back at the interview with Dr Ripley on pages 142-146 and say whether the following statements are true or false. Correct the false ones.

a. **Mammals have a well-defined colour sense.**

b. **Dillon Ripley was the youngest of the Ripley children.**

c. **The British had made a study of the fauna of the Arunachal Pradesh before Salim Ali and Ripley undertook the study.**

d. **In the 1930s, Salim Ali and Dillon Ripley made a survey of the fauna of the Deccan.**

e. **The reserve forests created by the British helped to preserve the bird species.**

f. The eucalyptus plantations can be harmful to the fauna of the region.

g. There is a greater danger of birds becoming extinct in India than in Europe.

h. Ripley and Salim Ali faced opposition from some local people.

i. The field work undertaken by Ripley took a long time. The preparation of the book was much quicker.

j. One of the hardships that Ripley had to bear was having to live in tents during the field work.

2. **Reading skills development**

Read this passage and complete the notes in the outline which follows it.

Animals at night

The animal kingdom can be divided into four categories. The first category comprises the diurnal animals, which are active during the day. In the second category, we have the nocturnal animals, which move about at night. Then we have two less well-known varieties, the crepuscular animals, which are active during twilight hours, and the arhythmic animals, which go about during both day and night. Probably such a division began when simple and weak animals began to come out in the dark to escape from diurnal predators. Today, although we associate the night with peace and silence, two-thirds of the mammals of the world move about at night, such mammals as mice, bats, foxes, flying squirrels and leopards.

How do the nocturnal animals find their way in the dark? Domestic cats, as we know, have eyes that can adapt to darkness. But in the wild, the mechanisms are more sophisticated. The eyes of an owl, for example, contain a large number of rods and nerve cells. These cells respond to dim light and to changes in light intensity. Would you believe it if you are told that an owl can detect a moving mouse in one-millionth of a candle power of light? Snakes make use of the sense of smell at night. Their tongue picks up small particles from objects around them and sensors at the roof of the mouth smell the particles. Another sense that helps animals to find their way is the sense of heat.

The snake, again, can record the heat emitted by objects around it and move in on the objects with deadly precision. Some animals have a sort of kinaesthetic sense which helps them to move about at night in familiar territory. It is a sense of the movements of the body involved in a particular action. Many of us walk down the stairs in the dark, open a cupboard and pick an object from inside with precision. It is this kind of sense that an owl uses to cover familiar territory. What do you know about a bat's ability to fly at night?

Most of us imagine that the main activities of animals at night consist of chasing and capturing their prey. To a certain extent this is true. Many animals seek and find their food at night. Owls pick up mice; tigers go out to feed upon animals which they have caught and stowed away earlier. But there are other activities at night. Animals play at night: raccoons, for example, play and gambol, as our pet dogs do in our garden. Male animals can be observed courting the females of their species. Spiders and toads court and mate at night: such behaviour has been observed by animal watchers.

But how does one watch animals in darkness? What are the techniques used for observing and taking pictures of animals at night? Any bright light will scare away the animals. Here scientists take advantage of the fact that most animals are blind to red light. They, therefore, use a torch with a red mask. Infra red telescopes have also ben used to observe animals at night. Today, with very sophisticated cameras and lighting devices, it is possible to photograph and make recordings of the cries of animals in their dark and inaccessible forest haunts.

Animals at night

A. ....

1. diurnal animals = ...
2. .... = ...
3. .... = out in twilight
4. .... = ...

B. ....

1. eyesight : ....
   ....
2. ....

3. sensitivity to heat : ....

....

4. ....

....

5. sound : ....

....

C. Activities at night ....

1. ....

2. ....

3. ....

D. ....

1. ....

2. ....

3. ....

3. Writing skills development

Using the notes given below, write a paragraph about lemmings.

lemmings - small rat-like creatures - inhabit Scandinavian mountains - population explosion once in three or four years - overcrowding - result : panic, aggression, mass migration downwards - fight, get killed, especially at barriers - advance - swim across small lakes - reach seashore: in Scandinavia mountain and sea close by - start swimming in the sea - get exhausted - drown - legend that lemmings commit suicide

4. Oral practice

Here are statements about snakes. Work in pairs and discuss whether the statements are true. Then tell the class whether you agree or disagree with each statement.

a. Snakes are slimy creatures.

b. The majority of snakes are very poisonous.

c. Snakes are very aggressive and will attack anyone who passes by.

d. Snakes use their tongue to smell objects.

e. Snakes dance to the sound of the snake-charmer's pipe.

f. Snakes can be tamed and kept as pets.

g. If a snake is cut into two, the two pieces will become two snakes.

h. Snakes reproduce by laying eggs.

i. A snake can swallow a prey that is many times its own size.

j. Cobras spit venom into the eyes of their enemies.

Industry Unit 1

Personnel and production

Preparation

1. **Oral practice**

a. In the following pairs of words, you find the sounds /v/ and /w/ . Practise the words with your partner till the distinction becomes clear.

verse, worse	vary, wary
veal, wheel	vile, while
vine, wine	veil, wail

b. In the following words /v/ and /w/ occur in the middle of the words. Practise these words with your partner.

coward, covered	reward, revolve
away,avail	rower, rover

c. In the following words you find the combination /kw/. Practise the words with your partner.

queen
quick
queer
equipment

d. How do you pronounce the words *woman* and *women* ? Check with your teacher.

e. In the letter on the next page find other words which have a /v/, /w/ or /kw/ sound. Write them down and practise with your partner.

2. **Writing skills development**

a. Letters constitute an important type of communication between individuals, between individuals and companies and between companies. A student completing his course of study will begin to look for employment, and at that time he will have to write letters applying for jobs. Here is a letter of application for a position in a plastics manufacturing company. Note the different parts of the letter.

100 Cathedral Road
Madras 600006
17 August 1987

To
The General Manager
India Plastics Ltd
Madras 600004

Dear Sir,

I should like to be considered for the position of sales engineer which you advertised in the Indian Express of 16 August

I passed the B.E.degree examination in mechanical engineering from Anna University in 1984. I passed the examination in the first class and was first among the successful candidates of the year. Earlier, in 1980, I passed the Higher Secondary School examination of the Tamil Nadu Board of Examinations in the first class.

Since July 1984, I have been employed as Supervisor in Madras Plastics and Chemicals in Ambattur. I have acquired a thorough knowledge of the manufacturing processes and marketing strategies for plastics products.

During my study in college I was a member of the National Service Scheme (NSS) for three years. I attended three NSS camps and along with other volunteers, took part in social service programmes.

I am 24 years old, my date of birth being 20 June 1963.

Mr K Sathyanarayana, General Manager of Madras Plastics Industries,Ambattur, Madras 600049 has agreed to be a referee on this application and will give you any information you may require regarding my service with his company.

I hope you will consider my application favourably.

Yours faithfully

V. Krishnamurthy

V KRISHNAMURTHY

Encl.

(Transcripts for academic study completed)
(Testimonial from the Principal of college last attended)

Now write a similar letter applying to any firm you are interested in, giving information about yourself. Discuss your letter with your partner and your partner's letter also. Would you give your partner the job? Would your partner give you the job? Be ready to report this to the class.

b. You will notice that in the above letter the applicant has written about his education, experience, extracurricular activities; he has named a referee who can supply information about him to the company.

Nowadays one is often expected to give details about oneself in an easy-to-read form. This statement is called biodata or personal data sheet. Here is a simple data sheet: transfer the details from the letter to the appropriate places in the data sheet.

Application for the post of

Personal Data

Name(Mr/Mrs/Miss)
Address
Age & date of birth

EDUCATION

Institution	Year	Examination	Class/Division and Rank

EXPERIENCE

Name of organisation	Period	Position held

EXTRACURRICULAR ACTIVITIES

REFERENCE

Some companies have printed forms for personal data. Details like marital status, state of health, hobbies , and memberships of clubs or professional bodies, are sometimes included in the biodata. In the next lesson, you will fill up a form of this kind.

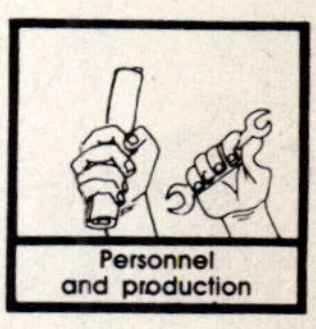

Part 1

1. **Language focus** — 'Units of measurement'

   a. Look at the following expressions.

The pipe is 3 feet long.
a 3-foot pipe

The curing lasts 60 minutes.
a 60-minute curing cycle

Note that when the numerical expression is placed in the position of an adjective before the noun, the singular form is used; the plural forms *feet* and *minutes* are not used. Now rewrite the following expressions as shown above.

a flask with a capacity of 10 litres
a journey of 20 miles
a match lasting five days
at intervals of ten minutes
a DC supply of 240 volts
a lamp of a power of 60 watts
an investment of Rs 350,000
a research grant of Rs 2 lakhs
pipes having an i.d. (internal diameter) of 3 inches

b. You are familiar with some of the abbreviations used for the names of units of measurement. Write out in full each of the expressions below.

3000 rev/ min
6.28 m/s
1500 kg/m^3
150 rpm
40 % v/v
15 psi
273 K
300 ppm
530 kHz
500 Btu/ft^3

2. **Reading** — 'The dry cell battery'

Read the following passage and find out the main ideas discussed by the writer. Then divide the passage into four paragraphs.

The dry cell battery has long been a familiar object in our homes. Its main use was to supply power for torch lights. The demand was stagnant for many years, and it was only with the introduction of portable radios and tape recorders that the manufacture of dry cell batteries became a profitable industry. Today dry cells of different sizes are used in transistor radios, calculators, portable tape recorders, quartz clocks and torches. The international sports events like Wimbledon and the World Cup series in cricket have increased the demand for dry cell batteries. Indian industrialists have been quick to foresee the increase in the demand for dry cell batteries and today the market for dry cell batteries in India has reached an astounding Rs 300 crore mark. The market leader is Eveready which commands nearly 50 per cent of the sales. Nippo and Novino each commands a little less than a quarter of the market. These three together with Toshiba and Geep constitute the major brands in the industry. Though the promise held by the dry cell industry seems to be bright, there are problems. The most serious of these is the fact that the installed capacity in the industry is far in excess of the demand. When the transistor was introduced in the 1960s, the increase in demand for dry cells was so sudden and so exciting that entrepreneurs enthusiastically set up units, small and big, for the manufacture of dry cells. Besides the five major manufacturers there are a dozen small industrialists. Some of the manufacturers have obtained technology from advanced countries and invested heavy amounts as capital. As against a demand for about 1200 million cells, the installed capacity is about 2000 million cells. This is the problem facing the industry. What are the prospects for the future ? The major units are engaged in severe competition spending large amounts of money in the promotion of their products through advertisements in the media. The smaller units find it hard to face up to such high-pressure, promotional strategies. They may find it difficult to survive, unless there is some technological development that leads to a repetition of the boom witnessed in the 1960s.

a. Mark the places where the passage can be divided into paragraphs.

b. Make a statement of the topic of each paragraph in one sentence.

c. Pick out the main points of each paragraph and write them down in note form.

d Which of the paragraphs contain factual information? Which of them contain opinions or suppositions, or statements of cause-and-effect.?

3. **Writing** — 'Report on the annual general meeting'

a. Look at the following pairs of sentences .

ia. The chairman said, 'Your company has done very well this year, and the profit before tax has risen from last year's Rs 80 lakhs to 120 lakhs this year.'

ib. The chairman said that the company had done very well during the year under report and the profit before tax had risen from the previous year's Rs 80 lakhs to Rs 120 lakhs during the current year.

iia. The chairman said, 'The company has not been able to achieve its production target this year.'

iib. The chairman admitted that the company had not been able to achieve its production target during the year under report.

iiia. The chairman said 'The unions have taken a hostile stand this year and production has been hit by repeated strikes.'

iiib. The chairman complained that the unions had taken a hostile stand during the year and production had been hit by repeated strikes.

Note the verbs used in the above examples to report the words of the chairman : *said*, *admitted* , *complained*. There are many other words of this kind which you can use in reporting speeches. Some of them are *explained*, *confessed*, *denied*, *replied*, *attributed*. Complete the following sentences in the same way using the above words.

iva. The chairman said, 'The project in Saudi Arabia has been the main cause of the drain on our funds.'

ivb. The chairman explained ....

....

va. The chairman said, 'Your company has been forced to resort to heavy borrowing during the year, and the rates of interest are very high.'

vb. The chairman confessed ....

....

via. The chairman said, 'The unit to be started in Mysore will be able to benefit from several incentives and backward area concessions offered by the Karnataka Government.'

vib. The chairman replied ....

....

viia. The chairman said, 'The customs officials have not extended to us the concessions available for imported components.'

viib. The chairman attributed ....

....

b. The passage given below is a record of the proceedings of the annual general meeting (AGM) of a company. After the chairman's speech, the shareholders of the company ask questions and the chairman replies to the questions. Prepare a report of the chairman's speech, and the questions and answers.

> **Chairman** : I have great pleasure in welcoming you, the shareholders of the company, to this annual general meeting. During the year that ended on 31st March 1986, your company's performance was satisfactory, though it failed to rise to your expectations. A number of adverse factors in combination worked to the detriment of the company. The situation in the cement units was grave, with three months being lost owing to labour trouble. The strike was unwarranted, and the cement units which were already in deep trouble received a crippling blow from the stoppage of work.

Another reason for the low profitability of the performance this year is the delay in the implementation of the cement project in Saudi Arabia. The plant is ready to go into operation, but there have been many technical hitches and the plant cannot be switched on till clearance from the Saudi government is received.

Although there is no room for panic or alarm in the company's performance, I am afraid the company is not in a position to declare a dividend this year. The plant in Saudi Arabia will go into operation within a few months and we have orders on hand to ensure profitability in the first year itself.

Ladies and gentlemen, I thank you for attending this meeting, which I consider a gesture of your support to and faith in the company.

A shareholder : How can you say that the performance of the company is satisfactory when there has been a loss of Rs 250 lakhs this year as against an average profit of Rs 2 crores in the previous years?

Chairman : The project in Saudi Arabia has been the main cause of the drain on our funds. Heavy investment has already been made and the project has come to a standstill, in fact, it cannot even take off on account of technical and procedural hurdles. Your company has been forced to resort to heavy borrowing during the year, and the rates of interest are very high. But once the Saudi project goes on stream, there will be quick results.

A shareholder : There is no strike in the electronics unit in Gujarat, but even there you have reported a loss. Can you explain why?

Chairman : Here again, the problem has been in the interpretation of the rules. The customs officials have not extended to us the concessions available for imported components. Their view is that these are not components, but are parts of complete units in unassembled condition. We have taken up this question with higher authorities. The practice seems to vary from port to port, and this has been pointed out.

A shareholder : You are planning to start a new unit for manufacture of electronics items in Mysore. I do not understand why a new unit should be started when you have already established electronics units in seven states.

Chairman : The unit to be started in Mysore will be able to benefit from several incentives and backward area concessions offered by the Karnataka government. Production can start within a few months and so the funds will not be locked up.

A shareholder : Do you think you will be able to declare a dividend next year?

Chairman : I am optismistic. Many units where work was held up will start production again very soon. I am confident that the coming year will show an upward trend in our turnover and profits.

Your report can begin thus:

The chairman welcomed the shareholders to the annual general meeting of the company. He said that the performance of the company for the year that ended on 31 March 1986 was satisfactory though .....

Personnel and production

Part 2

1. **Reading** — 'The state of the Indian tea industry'

Read the following passage and answer the questions at the end of it.

TEA has been in the headlines with *apprehensions* over shortage of supplies for domestic consumption pushing up prices by about 60 per cent in recent months. The output of this *beverage* had been rising regularly over a period from 569 million kg in 1980 to an all time high of 700 million kg in 1988. But the increase in output by 131 million kg has been helpful only in meeting the growth in internal consumption to 479 million kg from 345 million kg in eight years. Exports have been *fluctuating* around 200 million kg, there being actually a slight drop from 224 million kg in 1980 to 221 million kg in 1988. The needs of the domestic market have been increasing by five per cent annually and the output of tea would have to rise by 20-25 million kg yearly if exports have to be maintained at least around 200 million kg.

Changed situation

The present situation is in complete contrast with the conditions that prevailed in the fifties. The output of tea was 275 million kg in 1950 and exports 200 million kg with internal consumption accounting for 75 million kg. Even in 1960 the share of exports was 193 million kg out of a total output of 321 million kg, the quantity absorbed by the domestic market being 128 million kg. The intake of this beverage has been rising at a faster rate in recent years with an increase in the standard of living and the uptrend is likely to be more pronounced if the gross domestic product rose by an average of six per cent annually in the Eighth Plan. Any *shortfall* in domestic output may therefore necessitate a cutback in exports if an undue rise in prices for several grades is to be prevented. But the world supply situation also determines the fluctuations in prices as the developing countries dependent on imports have been increasing their purchases with an improvement in the gross national income. Thus world exports have been rising in spite of static trends being noticeable in some developed regions.

Irregular trend in output

The unexpected happenings in the latter half of 1989 were on account of fears about a shortfall in production, as stated above, by 10 million kg to 690 million kg in 1989 from 700 million kg in 1988. If the uptrend noticed in earlier years had been sustained, the yield should have been around 730 million kg. An irregular trend has been noticeable only in recent years as there was a dip in output to 624 million kg in 1986 from 657 million kg in 1985. These trends perhaps indicate that more vigorous efforts are needed for implementing the replantation programme and extending acreage under tea bushes wherever feasible in order to ensure that the target of 1,000 million kg by 2000 is realised. The export earnings are estimated at Rs 750 crores in 1989. There should not be any let up in the export effort as the overall trade gap is large in spite of a *spectacular* rise in total exports. It has of course to be made sure that production increases by at least 25-30 million kg yearly and even more for meeting fully not only increasing domestic consumption but also maintaining exports at least around the present levels.

The managements of tea estates are of course endeavouring to market common teas in limited quantities at a price of Rs 40 a kg on the suggestion of the Government. But the quantity involved is not more than 15 million kg and the lower priced packets may not be available fully to the low income groups if open market prices remained at higher levels. It was even suggested at one stage that common teas should be imported for meeting domestic requirements and higher value teas exported for maximising foreign exchange earnings. But this proposal has rightly been rejected by the Government. It will have to be examined, however whether exports could be effected on a more dispersed basis with a greater proportion of 'made up' teas for securing higher value added. The Soviet Union is the major buyer now *accounting for* nearly 50 per cent of total exports.

The tea industry is now having a spell of prosperity due to the upsurge in prices though the state governments tend to gain to a greater extent than the tea estates because of the heavy incidence of agricultural income tax. A good portion of the exceptional profits now being derived should be allowed to be utilised for executing replantation programmes and extending the area under tea. The States concerned should provide necessary incentives for maximising tea production with the Centre also making the requisite gestures. As there is a shortage of world supplies by 100 million kg and India is the largest producer, it has to formulate plans for increasing its output to 740-750 million kg in 1990. Otherwise there will have to be a sharp cutback in exports, and a *boom* in world prices. This situation should be prevented as the production should be raised to meet not only the growing need of the domestic consumers, but also those of export markets. The tea industry has a bright future and the opportunity for increasing output, *turnover* and profits in the nineties should be fully utilised.

a. You can get a clear idea of the trends in the production and export of tea if you tabulate the data. Complete the following table using the data available .

Year	Total output	Domestic Consumption	Export
	(quantities in million tonnes)		
1950			
1960			
1980			
......			
1985			
1986			
......			
1988			
1989			

Find out from the table in which year there was a reversal in the trend in total output of tea in the country.

b. The table shows that from 1980 to 1988

i. total production and domestic consumption increased, but exports fell.

ii. total production fell, domestic consumption fell, and exports increased.

iii. total production, domestic consumption and exports increased.

c. In paragraph 2, what reason does the author give for the increase in domestic consumption of tea?

   Does he believe that it will continue to increase?

d. In paragraph 4, the author refers to a curious step suggested for meeting the increased domestic demand. What is it?

e. What are the 'unexpected happenings' referred to at the beginning of paragraph 3?

f. How can India increase its output of tea?

2. **Writing** — 'Letter of application'

   Look at the advertisement given below.

> **Lucas-TVS**
>
> We are leaders in auto electricals
> with over 3000 employees and require
>
> DESIGN ENGINEERS
> for Special Purpose Machines
>
> Candidates should be mechanical
> engineering graduates — preferably with
> postgraduation in machine design. They
> should
>
> ... have a minimum of 5 years' experience in
> designing special purpose machines
> pertaining to metal cutting/metal
> forming/assembly machines for light
> precision work.

... be capable of independently designing SPMs from concept stage
... have knowledge of low cost automation.

Salary and service conditions would be attractive and not a restricting factor for the right candidate.

Please apply with complete bio-data, salary last drawn/salary expected and a brief description of the most interesting machine designed, within 15 days, superscribing the envelope with the position applied for, to

The Personnel Manager
Lucas-TVS Limited
Padi, Madras 600 050.

a. When you send an application in reply to the advertisement, you should carefully consider the qualifications and experience the company has specified. If you are sure that you possess these, you should write a letter of application.

100 Second Line Beach
Madras 600001
25 August 1987

The Personnel Manager
Lucas-TVS Limited
Padi, Madras 600050

Dear Sir,

I should like to be considered for the position of Design Engineer which you advertised in The Hindu of 16 August 1987.

I am enclosing my biodata sheet which shows that I have the qualifications prescribed by you. My specialisation in my undergraduate course was machine design, and my experience with

Madras Machine Works has enabled me to acquire a sound knowledge of special purpose machines.

I. should be grateful if you could grant me an interview in the next few days.

Yours faithfully

P. S. Narayan

P S NARAYAN

Enclosure:
Biodata

b. Prepare the biodata to be sent with this letter. Use the form given below.

BIODATA

Name

Address

Sex

Date of birth

Place of birth

EDUCATION

Institution	Dates	Diploma Degree	Subjects	Scholastic standing

Prizes, medals, awards won

EXTRACURRICULAR ACTIVITIES

EXPERIENCE

Company	Dates	Position held	Duties

PRESENT SALARY

HOBBIES

REFERENCES (names, positions and addresses of two referees)

1.

2.

DATE SIGNATURE

3. **Listening** — 'A process to make washing soap'

You will listen to a description of a process by which washing soap can be made at home. Take notes of things required for making soap and write about the process in the form of a set of instructions.

a. Things required for making soap

i. ....

ii. ....

....

....

....

....

b. Process in the form of a set of instructions

i. ....

ii. ....

....

....

....

....

Follow-up

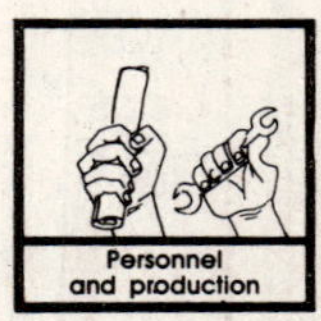

1. **Language development**

Here are some important rules for writing the SI (Systeme Internationale) units.

a. SI units must always be written in upright roman letters.

b. Plural -*s* is not added to the units.

e.g. 6 metres should be written 6 m and not 6 ms.
6 ms stands for 6 milliseconds.

c. A fullstop is not used after the symbol.

d. The multiplication sign is not used between units; a space is left between them.

e. Prefixes like m (milli) or c (centi) must be written close to the unit in small letters.

e.g. cm (centimetre)
mN (millinewton)

f. The solidus (/) should not be used twice in the derived unit.

e.g. metre per second per second is written
m/s^2 NOT m/s/s

Note that temperature is measured in K (Kelvin) in SI units. But for everyday temperature measurement Celsius is used. Look at the following equation: how does Celsius representation differ from Kelvin representation?

The coefficient of linear expansion is

$12 \times 10^{-6}/°C$ or
$12 \times 10^{-6}/K$

Correct the mistakes in the following representations of SI units:

1 m = 100 cms
Acceleration = 9.8 m/s/s
Freezing point of water = 273°K
Radius of the earth = 6378 kms.
I w = 1 N.m/sec

2. Language check

The prefixes *infra-* and *sub-* are added to words to mean 'below, lower down'; the prefixes *super-*, *supra-*, *ultra-* and *hyper-* are intensifying prefixes, which mean 'above, higher up, beyond'.

Add one of these prefixes to the following words to give the meanings given against them:

........conductivity: the property of having zero electrical resistance

........violet: having wavelength beyond the violet end of the spectrum

........zero: less than zero

........red: having wavelength just below the red end of the spectrum

........sensitive: abnormally or excessively sensitive

........heat: heat above boiling point without causing vaporisation

........sonic: (sound waves) just below the level of audibility

........saturate: add to solution beyond saturation point

........continent: large land mass, not large enough to be called continent

........sonic: having a speed greater than that of sound

........national: going beyond or above national limits or national considerations

........standard: not having the required or normal quality

........sonic: (sound) having a pitch above the upper limit of human hearing

........tension: abnormal blood pressure

........structure: subordinate or underlying parts on which something is built

3. Reading skills development

In the following passage, you will read about an industrial process. After reading the passage, answer the questions.

Spread over five hectares, the joint Indo-U.S. plant is located in one of the most industrially backward areas of Andhra Pradesh. But it is an area rich in high-quality clay — the main raw material in the manufacture of quality ceramic tiles.

The clay used by Spartek is really sediment deposits which collect at the bottom of irrigation tanks and village ponds. 'Most villages in this region,' says Tripuraneni, the managing director of Spartek Ceramics, 'have irrigation tanks that fill up during the rainy season. During the summer months the rainwater is used by the people, leaving behind fine red clay. In mining this clay, we also help desilt the tanks for use by the farmers again.'

'The clay is just right for the making of tiles. It has the right strength, the right plasticity — in fact all the essential properties that CeramicUS insisted it must have to make first-rate tiles.'

The mined clay is brought to the Tirupati plant and mixed with other ingredients in a ball mill and wet-ground into a fine slip. The slip is then stored for a few days and spray dried to form a fine powder of uniform consistency so that, when it is compressed in a 680-ton press, it maintains its homogeneity. The massive press gives the tiles the required strength, shape and thickness.

From the press the tiles are sent along a 90-metre-long glazing line, where they acquire surface finish, and where the requisite designs are screen-printed.

From the glazing line the tiles are automatically fed into specially designed rail trolleys. The trolleys take the tiles to the head of an 84-metre-long kiln.

The massive kiln is the heart of the tile-making operation. Inside it rages a ball of fire — at 1,200 degrees

Celsius! It bakes about 2,000 tiles a day, and each tile takes an hour to reach the other end of the kiln on a belt of 1,680 rollers. And throughout the 60-minute curing cycle, operators closely monitor the tiles on closed-circuit television to ensure that each one is fired to just the right degree.

'The kiln is crucial to the whole process,' Tripuraneni points out. 'Normally tiles in India are baked in a tunnel kiln in which the firing time is somewhere in the range of 72 hours. In our kiln, it is just an hour. CeramicUS, which has the same kiln, uses even less time — a 30-minute cycle for certain kinds of tiles.'

The Spartek kiln is by all accounts the most advanced of its kind. It uses liquefied petroleum gas (LPG), one of the cleanest fuels. 'Many tile plants in India run on furnace oil or coal, both of which affect the quality of tiles. Oil has sulphur in it and coal has tar and ash content which interfere with colour quality. Moreover, sulphur reacts with the chemicals used for glazing tiles, and this leaves a patchy effect and pinholes in the tiles. That is why most overseas manufacturers of tiles of international quality have switched over to gas-fired kilns.'

Another big advantage of an LPG kiln is its fuel efficiency. 'We save about 70 per cent in fuel expenditure, which is the single biggest cost component in tiles. In the manufacture of tiles roughly 50 per cent of the cost is accounted for by the fuel. This saving gives us a vital cost advantage.'

One leaves the Spartek plant amazed at how modern technology transforms a waste product – the lowly earth – into tiles of exquisite beauty and a joy for the modern home or office.

(Source: *Span*)

a. Note the various steps in the process of tile making. Draw a flow chart representing these steps.

b. Why was this region in Andhra Pradesh selected for the location of the plant?

c. *Complete the following sentences.*

   i. The function of the glazing line is to ....

   ii. The function of the ball mill is to ....

   iii. The function of the kiln is to ....

   iv. The function of the press is to ....

   In what order are these functions performed in the process of tile making?

d. Make a comparison of the Spartek kiln with the kilns normally used for tile making in India. Complete the following table:

	feature	Spartek kiln	other kilns
i			
ii			
iii			
iv			

Industry Unit 2

Safety and training

Preparation

1. Oral practice

a. *Saftey First !* This is the motto that people working in laboratories and factories must bear in mind. In our homes too, accidents can happen and we have to take precautions to prevent them.

In small groups, discuss the accidents that can happen in the chemistry laboratory. Note them down and think of the safety rules that must be observed. Tell the class about the danger and about the rules to be observed. Here is an example.

> There is a likelihood of pieces of glass being scattered on the floor. Acids too may be spilt on the floor.
>
> DO NOT WORK IN THE LABORATORY BAREFOOT. WEAR SHOES TO PROTECT YOUR FEET.

Find as many other safety rules as you can. Here are some hints to set you thinking: clothes, gloves, labels on bottles transferring liquids, mixing liquids, cuts, burns, suffocation, explosion, gas cylinders.

b. What are the following things used for? Why are they known by these names?

safety pin	safety razor	safety lock
safety belt	safety lamp	safety valve

2. Writing skills development

Here are some instructions you often come across. Where do you find them? Pick out the instructions that refer to safety, and write a brief note on each of them. Write about where you find the instruction, what it means and why it is necessary.

> Keep out of the reach of children.
> Keep off the grass.
> Do not distract the driver.
> Write your name in block letters.
> No smoking!
> In case of emergency, break glass.
> Write nothing in the space below.
> For external use only.
> Do not pluck the flowers.
> Shake well before using.

3. Reading skills development

Read the following text and make notes on the important points in it.

The training of employees in a modern organisation is a process far different from what it was in the past. When a carpenter or a mason wanted to learn the skills of carpentry or masonry in the past, he would apprentice himself to an experienced craftsman and learn from him. Then for the rest of his life, he would keep working and earning his living using the skills he learnt from his master.

Today, training is given in institutes where the latest tools and methods are used in the training programme. The craftsman learns something of the theory behind the skills that he learns, instead of blindly doing what he was taught to do. Adaptation to new tools and methods is an important aspect of his training. With modern techniques, the employees can complete the work more quickly and more efficiently. The tedium of manual labour is to a considerable extent reduced. The training that the workers get makes them more receptive to change. They are willing to give up their age-old habits of work.

Employees are selected by organisations after an assessment of the skills they possess. Today, the process of training continues even after the selection is made. This is known as in-service training and is in many ways more important than pre-service training. This is because jobs are becoming more and more specialised. The purpose of such training is not merely to 'teach' the employees about new techniques to be adopted by them. It is equally intended to improve the morale of the workers. By participating in training programmes organised by the employer, the workers get a feeling that they are important, and that their employers care for them. They also become convinced of the dignity of labour and begin to take pride in what they are doing.

This brings us to another important aspect of training. This is the promotion of good interpersonal relations in the organisation. In the past, each worker was seen as an individual, isolated from the others. Today, the employers try to create a sense of fellowship among the workers. They are trained to work as a team and to submit to the discipline of a corporate life. Such training has become necessary because modern manufacturing processes call for the collective effort of a large number of people possessing various skills. Relations among the employees and relations between the employees and the management have to be good for the success of the enterprise. It is here that the industrial psychologist plays an important role. To the psychologist, the employee is not a cog in the wheel, but a human being who has emotions which have to be satisfied besides physical needs to be met. The psychologist has an important function in the organisation today. He pays attention to the psychological factors involved, both at the level of the individual and at the level of groups, and advises the management on the training programmes that would best promote the interests of the organisation, of both the employees and the management.

4. Language development

Supply the appropriate prepositions in the following sentences:

i. He drove the car .... a speed of 80 miles an hour.

ii. He was not prepared to act .... his principles.

iii. The factory has been closed .... two years.

iv. The road has a gradient of one .... six.

v. .... tomorrow evening, the report will be ready.

vi. Yesterday the chairman left .... New Delhi.

vii. The ball missed the goal .... inches.

viii. .... the last earthquake, the town has been facing many difficulties.

ix. The value was calculated .... an accuracy of three decimal places.

x. As the spaceship sailed .... Jupiter, it sent photographs of the planet to the earth station.

xi. The room measures 60 feet .... 40 feet.

xii. This motor consumes electricity .... 2 kilowatts per hour.

Part 1

1. **Reading** — 'A new safety device'

Read the following newspaper report.

> **Safety devices to detect leakage of current**
>
> MADRAS, Nov. 30.
>
> To protect the life and property from damage due to electrical accidents, the English Electric Co. of India has introduced two Residual Current Devices (RCDs.). Mr C.R. Balasubramanian, Managing Director, and Mr K.K. Gupta, Director (Hosur works) of the Company, told presspersons on Wednesday that these devices — Safe Trip and Super Trip — when attached to the mains would detect a leakage in current as low as 30 mA and immediately break the circuit, thereby preventing any accident. The RCDs can be used in residential buildings, high rise buildings, hotels, theatres, hospitals, laboratories, and industries.

Note the information contained in the report. Then look at the following advertisement. How are the report and advertisement related?

WHILE YOU ARE AWAY AT WORK, YOUR CHILD IS PLAYING WITH HIS LIFE !
In the eyes of electricity innocence does not touch a sentimental note. Imagine while you and your wife are away at work, the servant is busy in the kitchen, your innocent child could mistake a three pin socket for a toy. When this happens the apple of your eye will become a distant loving memory. It's childs play for electricity to strike a fatal blow!
English Electric brings to you a life saver, 'SAFE TRIP' Once fitted to the mains, this residual current device trips instantaneously at the slightest hint of current leakage, making your house a safe environment to live in.
Invest in a
ENGLISH ELECTRIC
SYMBOL OF EXCELLENCE
Safe-trip
Before it is too late!
INSTALLATION FREE IN MADRAS CITY AS SERVICE TO SOCIETY
Marketed by:
MULTI VISTA PRIVATE LIMITED
9, Fifth Main Road, Raja Annamalaipuram, Madras-600 028. Phone: 458357
AAA/MV/89134

Now answer the following questions:

i. What is the purpose of the report, and of the advertisement? To whom are the two addressed?

ii. Does the advertisement have more factual information than the report?

iii. How does the report describe the protection that the device gives? How does the advertisement describe it?

iv. Look at the left half of the advertisement. The picture there has three parts. What does each part do in communicating the message?

v. Describe the scene in the photograph, using the picture and then the first paragraph of the advertisement.

vi. Do you notice any difference in the style of the writing in the report and in the advertisement? Which sounds more personal and direct to you? Pick out the words that give you this impression.

2. **Role play** — 'A safety device'

Students A and B: You represent the company which manufactures the safety device mentioned in the previous task. Student A is the Managing Director and Student B is the Director (Hosur works). You will now be interviewed by two journalists. Read the report and the advertisement again.

Students C and D: You are journalists interviewing the spokespersons of the company manufacturing the safety device. Read the report and the advertisement and think of the questions that you would like to ask.

When all of you are ready, role-play the interview.

3. **Listening** — 'Safety measures in a chlorine plant'

You are now going to listen to a talk on 'Precautions to be taken in a chlorine plant'. As you listen, write down the relevant points in the outline provided.

Before you listen, prepare yourself by discussing with your neighbour the properties of chlorine that make it a dangerous gas.

Safety measures in the chlorine plant

- **Storing**
- **Handling**
- **Packing**
- **Employee selection**
- **Training**

Safety and training

4. **Writing** — 'An accident in the factory'

The Works Manager of Industrial Gases Limited has reported to the Chairman of the company that there has been an accident in the factory. Three workers in the gas filling section have been hospitalised after inhaling chlorine gas. The Chairman asks the Chief Engineer to conduct an inquiry into the accident and submit a brief report within two days.

Imagine that you are the Chief Engineer of the Company. Note down the points that should go into the report and then prepare the report. Divide it into paragraphs. Your report should contain answers to the following questions: Where? When? Who? What? How? and Why?

Safety and training

Part 2

1. **Discussion** — 'Employee training'

Answer the following questions. Work in pairs.

a. What are the objectives of imparting training to employees? Arrange the following in order of importance.

   i. increasing productivity
   ii. ensuring safety in the place of work
   iii. increasing the worker's earning capacity
   iv. promoting good interpersonal relations in the organisation
   v. preparing for the future

   Can you think of any other objective?

b. The following is a list of both conventional and unconventional methods of training. Which of them do you consider conventional?

   i. the audiovisual method
   ii. training through skits or songs
   iii. lectures
   iv. apprenticeship
   v. self-learning kits
   vi. games
   vii. case studies
   viii. quiz programmes
   ix. distance education

   Speak to the class briefly about one of the unconventional methods you are familiar with.

2. **Reading** — 'Training in industrial organisations'

Read the following passage and then answer the questions that follow.

Training forms the axle of the industrial wheel. It is an inevitable and continuous process in an industrial set-up, and no industrial organisation can function successfully without giving adequate training to its employees. C.R. Dooley, an American writer, while writing about training within industry, says, 'Training is not something that is done once to new employees — it is used continuously in every well-run establishment. Every time you get someone to do work the way you want it done, you are training. Every time you give directions or discuss a procedure, you are training.'

Training plays a vital role in industries because of the following reasons.

The newly appointed employees in any industry have to be trained to get themselves introduced to their new employer's work environment and to be taught to perform specific tasks.

Secondly, if an employee is promoted or is given new assignments, new skills must be developed.

Thirdly, even if an employee continues in the same job, he needs to be given training in order to update his technical know-how.

Fourthly, when the skill and ability of an employee is found to be inadequate for the particular area at the time of appraising his performance, he needs to be trained.

Fifthly, training is needed in order to make the employee cope with the changing goals of the organisation.

Any industrial organisation will definitely fail to achieve its ends if these training programmes are ineffectively conducted. The Organisation, the Trainer and the Trainee are the three key factors which contribute with equal importance to the effectiveness of training.

Every organisation employs various techniques and methods to give training to its employees. Case method, role play, lecture, films, incident method, problem-oriented exercises and projects, and programmed instruction are some of the very common methods adopted by the organisations. These methods vary according to the goals, structure and administrative practices of the organisation.

Apart from these, the learner's specific needs and his ability to understand and learn are the other factors which make the management think of other methods of training.

The primary aim of training in any industry is to educate and to help its personnel to rise up to certain standards to meet the factory's requirements. At the same time, some advantageous byproducts spring through training. They are prevention of accidents, averting damage to machinery and equipment, reduction of scrap generation, high quality production, increase in production, and better industrial relations.

a. Look at the above text as a whole. Do you think it is properly organised? Is it logically arranged and divided into appropriate paragraphs? Answer 'yes' or 'no'. Come back to this question after answering the remaining questions.

b. Which part of the text forms the introduction? What does the author do in the introduction?

c. Where does the second part of the text begin? Where does it end? Compare your answer with your neighbour's.

d. What does the author say in the next section?

e. Do you think the essay has a good conclusion? Can you write a different concluding section of your own?

f. The text has eleven paragraphs. Do you think it could do with fewer paragraphs? How would you reorganise the paragraphs?

3. **Writing** — 'A checklist on safety'

A checklist is a list of items that people use to make sure that everything is in order before any important activity is taken up. Here is a simple checklist: can you say when it can be used?

a.	Is there water in the radiator?	YES ☐	NO ☐
b.	Is there petrol in the tank?	YES ☐	NO ☐
c.	Are the brakes in good condition?	YES ☐	NO ☐
d.	Are the tyres properly inflated?	YES ☐	NO ☐
e.	Is the oil level in the engine right?	YES ☐	NO ☐

In the passage which follows, you will read some instructions regarding the construction of temporary structures like pandals, shamianas and tents. Pandals are often erected for public functions, cultural programmes, marriages and other events. The risk of fire in such structures is very high and, therefore, the Bureau of Indian Standards has suggested the following guidelines. Prepare a checklist for safety from these guidelines.

All combustible material used in the structure should be treated with fire retardant solution of ammonium sulphate, ammonium carbonate, borax, boric acid, alum and water in such proportion as specified in the Standard.

The main structure should be put up with at least 100 mm diameter wooden posts preferably of *sal*, casuarina or bamboo using lighter poles and trusses tied together with steel wire for the remaining structures.

The minimum height of the ceiling should not be less than three metres.

All fabrics, decorative material and coir ropes used in the construction and decoration of the temporary structure should be dipped in a fire retardant solution before use.

A clear space of three metres should be kept on all sides between the structure and adjacent buildings.

No temporary structure should be erected beneath live electrical lines or near furnaces, railway lines, electrical substations or chimneys.

All sides of the temporary structure should be kept open and, where it is not possible to do so, the lower portions of the side walls should not preferably be fixed.

There should also be provision for at least two separate, remotely located exits with their width determined on the basis of at least one unit of 50 cm for every 50 persons but not less than 1.5 m.

There should be a clear indication of the EXIT sign in plain legible letters and the exit light should be adequately illuminated with a reliable light source.

Temporary lighting of the structure should be installed by a licensed electrical engineer, and the load per circuit, insulation and the installation should conform to IS 1646 : 1982 Code of Practice for Fire Safety of Buildings (General): Electrical Installations.

Portable incandescent gas lights should be placed on securely fixed separate stands instead of being hung from the ceiling of the *pandal*. Can you think of any other items to be added to the checklist?

4. **Language focus** — 'Word formation'

You will find below a list of verbs. Two nouns can be formed from each verb, the first one referring to an action or state, and the second to a substance or material. The first line is completed for you. Supply nouns for the remaining verbs.

Verb	Noun 1	Noun 2
pollute	pollution	pollutant
explode	....	....
catalyse	....	....
disinfect	....	....
corrode	....	....
refrigerate	....	....
adhere	....	....
absorb	....	....
resist	....	....
react	....	....
detonate	....	....
stimulate	....	....
retard	....	....

Safety and training

Follow-up

1. **Comprehension check**

Go back to the text on pages 191 and 192. Answer the following questions.

a. How does C.R. Dooley's view of training differ from the view commonly held?

b. Look at the five reasons for training given in the text. Which of these apply to individual workers? Which of them refer to group training?

c. In India, industry has been asked to focus on rural areas. Which of the five reasons given by the author applies to this situation?

d. What is the need for training (i) a new employee, and (ii) an employee already in service?

e. What part can group discussion play in the training of employees?

f. Read the last paragraph again. How can training help in

— the prevention of accidents?
— the reduction of scrap generation?
— averting damage to machinery and equipment?

g. Outline a programme of training for a person who has just been selected as a management trainee. Discuss this with your neighbour and then write the outline.

2. **Reading skills development** — 'The detection of toxic gases'

Read the following description of an alarm system which detects the presence of dangerous gases like nerve gas and sends out a warning signal. Then label the diagram with the names of the parts of the system found in the text.

The air to be tested is drawn into the system by a *pump*. After passing through a *coarse filter* and a *fine filter*, the air enters a *chamber* with a *window* on one side. A *beam of light* from an *infrared source* falls on the air in the chamber through the

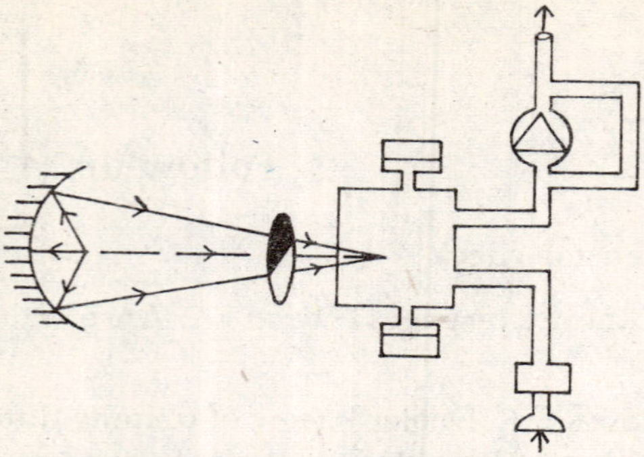

window. The light passes through a *rotating chopper*, with one half black. This turns the light into alternating bright and dim pulses. When any toxic gas is present in the chamber, it absorbs the infrared light and then the temperature in the chamber rises slightly. Consequently the pressure increases. But because the infrared light is in pulses, the pressure fluctuates with the same frequency. The fluctuation in pressure is turned into an acoustic wave. This acoustic is turned into a sound signal by the two *microphones* on the walls of the chamber.

The pump draws the air out of the chamber and releases it into the atmosphere through the *air outlet*.

3 Language check

Look at the list of words given below. Use these words to fill the blanks in the text that follows. Change the form of the words if necessary.

evaporate	contact	excessive
pulmonary	adopt	affect
occur	exposure	presence
copious	danger	build
attribute	react	increase

Chlorine gas is primarily a respiratory irritant. Restlessness, throat irritation, sneezing and .... salivation are the results of prolonged .... to the gas. In extreme cases, lung tissues may be .... resulting in severe .... diseases. If liquid chlorine is splashed on the eyes, skin, or clothing, it will cause irritation and chemical burns on the body.

Chlorine causes not only health hazards, but also explosion hazards. In the .... of sunlight, chlorine gas .... spontaneously and explosively with hydrogen to form hydrogen chloride. That is the reason why extreme precautionary measures must be .... during the manufacture of chlorine by electrolysis, failing which serious fire or explosion will ....

A similar explosion risk is involved in the case of liquid chlorine because it .... in volume when .... So there is always the .... of rupture of containers, pipelines and other equipment where chlorine is used, whenever .... pressure is .... up due to heat.

Fire hazard is another hazard .... to chlorine, as it may react to cause fire or explosions upon .... with turpentine, ether, ammonia, sawdust and phosphorus.

4. Writing skills development

Write a paragraph about the importance of computer training today. You can write about the use of computers by banks, travel agencies, railways, airlines, and business houses. Pay attention to the logical arrangement of the sentences of your paragraph.

Industry Unit 3

Selling products

Selling products

Preparation

1. Oral practice

Discuss the following questions in small groups. Be ready to report your ideas to the class when you are asked to.

a. What are the strategies of selling adopted today by firms to promote the sale of their products?

b. What do you think of the role of advertisement in the sale of products? What are the media involved for the purpose?

c. What do you think is the part played by exhibitions and fairs in promoting the sale of products?

d. Can you mention some Indian products for which there is a market in the other countries of the world?

2. Language development

Match the words in column A with their meanings in column B. Make sure you can pronounce all the words in column A correctly.

A	B
target	bind one (self) to a course of action
support price	system of services forming a basis
commitment	possible or probable customer
trade fair	objective, result aimed at
infrastructure	system of defending home industries
proposition	stipulated minimum amount of money to be paid for buying a commodity
statutory	a scheme suggested
prospect	periodical gathering for sale of goods at fixed place and time
protectionism	planning
projection	required by written law or legislation

constraint	seeing as a whole, and not in parts
impediment	limitation or restriction imposed forcibly
holistic	obstacle, hindrance

3. **Reading skills development**

   a. Read the passage quickly and say what its theme is.

   b. Read the passage again and indicate the place in it where there is a hint of a change.

When one looks at the European Community's relations with third world countries, one finds that, for historical and political reasons, the Community and most of its member states have continued to pay preferential attention to North Africa and the Asian countries. India with its relatively slow rate of growth, monetary conservatism and 'muddling' bureaucracy did not appear as exciting or exotic as the others. Of late, events in other regions and India's own recent performance have highlighted the virtues of consistency, stability through democracy, and change through continuity. The Community has acknowledged the pace of these events by establishing its own Mission in India. The Mission already has notable successes to its credit in broadening awareness and fostering deeper understanding of mutual benefits from more effective cooperation between India and the Community.

4. **Writing skills development**

An instruction tells you what you should or should not do. A warning informs you beforehand of a danger to come.

Write down as many instructions or warnings as you are likely to find on the following. An example (a) is given.

a. a packet of cigarettes .... Cigarette smoking is injurious to health.

b. a container of chemicals ....

c. a bottle of medicine ....

d. a packet of fragile material such as glass ....

e. a film roll ....

f. a tube of ointment ....

Part 1

1. **Discussion** — 'Trade balance'

Discuss the following questions in small groups. Be ready to report to the class when asked to do so.

a. What do you understand by the expression trade balance'?
b. What measures do you think need to be adopted in order for us to have a favourable trade balance?
c. What do you know about the present state of India's foreign trade?
d. What do you understand by the expressions 'buyer's market' and 'seller's market'?
e. What do you know about the EEC and its relations with India?

2. **Reading** — 'India and the E.E.C.

Read the following passage and answer the questions at the end of it.

India and the EEC

i. When one looks at the European Community's relations with third world countries, one finds that, for historical and political reasons, the Community and most of its Member states have continued to pay preferential attention to North Africa and the Asian countries. India with its relatively slow rate of growth, monetary conservatism and 'muddling' bureaucracy did not appear as exciting or exotic as the others. Of late, events in other regions and India's own recent performance have highlighted the virtues of consistency, stability through democracy, and change through continuity. The Community has acknowledged the pace of these events by establishing its own Mission in India. The Mission already has notable successes to its credit in broadening awareness and fostering deeper understanding of mutual benefits from more effective cooperation between India and the Community.

ii. As India pursues its objective of modernising its economy, the opportunity for the Community's technological and financial inputs expands. India's Seventh Five Year Plan postulates an investment of nearly Rs 3500 billion during 1985-90. Such vital sectors as energy, transport, communications, agro-chemicals and heavy industry have programmes for significant capacity expansion and modernisation. Businessmen and bankers from the Member States have shown great interest in these programmes. The current economic environment in India permits freer imports of technology and equipment. Freer inflow of capital, know-how and know-why from Western Europe can help nourish a new crop of joint ventures and raise the level of economic transactions to new heights.

iii. For the full potential to be realised, the existing imbalances and asymmetries will have to be rectified. EEC is the most important of India's trading partners accounting for nearly 23 per cent of India's exports and 20 per cent of imports. The share of Indian exports in the EC market is, however, a low 0.28 per cent. The Community's surplus in trade with India is mounting rapidly. Its protectionist policies, especially in agriculture and textiles, constrain further expansion of Indian exports to Western Europe. With the admission of Spain and Portugal into the Community, pressures for intensifying protectionist measures may increase. Aggravation of current constraints would spell disaster for the inviting prospects now looming on the horizon. A positive approach is called for to reverse the negative trend.

iv. Several constructive suggestions are on the anvil. These include review and relaxation of GSP measures, extension of Indo-EEC joint ventures to third countries and collaboration to improve agricultural productivity in sub-Saharan countries. But without a wider vision, a holistic approach, and a determined drive, the expectations aroused may be only partially fulfilled.

v. Paucity of adequate information about investment opportunities, economic policies, resource endowments and technological capability continues to be a serious impediment. Firms, government officials and, most important, influential citizens lack adequate knowledge of conditions in the two regions. Some significant steps to dispel ignorance have been taken in recent years. The Festival of India in Paris, India's participation at the Hanover Fair as a partner country, conferences and seminars sponsored by the Indo-EEC Joint Commission, etc., have fostered a positive image and mutual comprehension. Much more remains to be done.

(Indrama XII (1) 35-36 by K.B. Lall)

i. This passage mentions a problem faced by India and refers to possible solutions. Where is the problem first mentioned?

ii. Can you find a transition in the first paragraph from statement of a problem to a hint at a solution? Which words introduce the transition?

iii. Choose one of the following as a possible statement of the topic of the second paragraph.

   a. Lack of understanding of India among the members of the EEC
   b. Opportunities for EEC investment in India
   c. India's impressive growth in modernising its economy.

iv. Explain the difference between the following two statements (paragraph iii):

   a. EEC accounts for 23 per cent of India's exports.
   b. The share of Indian exports in the EC market is a low 0.28 per cent.

v. Which of the following are mentioned in the passage as reasons for the trading pattern between India and the EEC countries?

   a. India's export policy
   b. Import policy of EEC countries
   c. Sub-standard quality of Indian products
   d. Preferential treatment given by EEC to some other countries
   e. Lack of information about opportunities in India for EEC countries

vi. Find words in the passage having the following meanings. The first letter and the paragraph number are given.

c............................... (i) : maintenance of a state of affairs without change

p..................................... (ii) : supporting home industry against competition from other countries

s........................... (i) : quality of being firmly fixed or established c.................................. (iii) : limitation or restriction imposed forcibly

i.. (v) : obstacle, hindrance

h........................ (iv) : seeing as a whole, and not in parts

c.. (v) : understanding

3. **Listening** — 'Export commitment of the FICCI'

You are going to listen to a talk about the export commitment of the Federation of Indian Chamber of Commerce and Industry (FICCI). Listen carefully for the details and take notes of as many of them as you can on the lines indicated below.

a. The occasion for the commitment ....

b. The nature of the commitment ....

c. The percentage of the business houses to be committed which are already major exporters ....

d. The projected increase in foreign exchange earnings as per this commitment by 1989-90 ....
by 1991-92 ....

e. Projected industrial exports
by 1989-90 ....
by 1991-92 ....

f. The condition on which this projection is based ....

g. The conditions for achieving export success ....

h. The state of the present trade balance ....
The important factor deciding it ....

i. The projected increase in imports
by 1989-90 ....
by 1991-92 ....

j. The increase in exports that would be needed to match this level of imports ....

4. **Writing** — 'India s foreign trade and export ratios'

You will find below two tables showing the figures of India's foreign trade and India's export ratios. These have been taken from the issue of *Business India* July 27-August 9, 1987. Study these tables.

Table 1
India's foreign trade

	(Rs crores)			
	Year ending March			
	1961	1971	1985	1987
Imports	1,140	1,634	17,171	20,063
Exports	660	1,535	11,855	12,550
Trade Balance	(–) 480	(–) 99	(-) 5,316	(-) 7,513

Table 2
India's export ratios

	India's exports as a percentage of		
Year	World exports	India's Imports	India's national income
1949	2.40	—	—
1961	1.05	57.9	5.0
1971	0.65	93.9	4.5
1985	0.43	69.0	6.8
1987	0.40	62.6	6.6

Now write a paragraph indicating what the figures in Table 1 convey. If you finish early and if you have time, write another paragraph similarly in respect of Table 2.

Selling products

Part 2

Reading — 'Direct marketing'

a. i. Look at the title of the following passage. Discuss with another student what you think it means.

ii. Now write down six words which you expect to see in the passage. Can you predict what the passage is likely to say?

iii. Now read the passage and check whether the words you chose in ii appeared or not. Which words might have appeared but did not?

iv. Did the passage say what you predicted?

b. Now read the passage again and make brief notes on the lines suggested below.

i. Ways of advertising possible according to the text.

a. ....

b. ....

ii. Their relative merits and demerits ....

iii. The basis of direct marketing ....

iv. Its feasibility in India ....

v. The features of an effective mailing list

a. ....

b. ....

c. ....

d. ....

vi. The success of the direct mail rests on

a. ....

b. ....

c. ....

Direct Marketing

The use of the national media to advertise products is a sheer waste of money and effort when not many people are interested. There must be some other way of getting past these people and reaching one's specific target audience.

Direct marketing is big business in the US. Here in India, the idea is yet to catch on. Direct mail, an example of this kind of marketing, has been taken up by advertising agencies though grudgingly; the concept as yet remains half-baked. The infrastructure required is non-existent at present. Yet the Indian market with its expanding industrial base and thousands of medium and small scale manufacturers cannot afford to ignore the potential and possibilities of such a marketing tool.

At the heart of any direct marketing effort is the mailing list — comprehensive, up-to-date, non-duplicated and accurate.

To assure the most effective use of the mailing list, an important question would be to ask which names on the lists are the best prospects. A mailing list that can continuously answer this question is an invaluable asset.

Avoiding duplication while compiling the list and ensuring accuracy are essential. A misspelt name is a sure way of affronting a prospect apart from the fact that it often causes delay in situations when time is crucial.

Direct mail material can be of many forms and styles. Whatever the style, boldness and brevity are the keynotes of any attractive offer. This alone will help prevent the flight of the mail to the waste paper basket. The next most important thing is to saturate the mail with the various advantages and benefits of your product so that there will be something to interest every reader.

Even after all the interest has been generated and desire kindled, the aim of direct mailing is hardly complete without that all-important reply or action provoking response advice. It is on this mainspring that the delicate balance between success or failure of the direct mail rests.

(Adapted from 'Reaching out from Business to Business', *Technocrat*, June 1987.)

2. **Writing** — 'K'86 fair in Dusseldorf'

You will find below an outline of an event in the form of disjointed hints. Develop it into a paragraph.

K'86 fair - Dusseldorf - West Germany - World's largest plastic and rubber fair - record number of 220,000 visitors from 111 countries-over 3000 Indian visitors - participants - 1700 exhibitors from 40 countries - official Indian participation - 13 exhibitors - organised by the Trade Fair Authority of India - good business of some companies reported - PVC leather cloth, plastic electrical components, laminated sheets, PVC films, packaging boards, flasks and advertising materials fared well - Indo-German Chamber of Commerce - organisation of - buyer-seller meet during the fair - 26 German firms participants - their keen interest in Indian goods.

3. **Reading** — 'Buyer's bible'

a. Discuss the following questions in small groups. Be ready to report to the class when you are asked to.

   i. What is meant by quality control with reference to products for sale?

   ii. Are you familiar with the concept of consumer movement?

   iii. Are you aware of any consumer movement in India?

b. Read the following text and compare your answers to (a) with the text.

Americans shop for everything from food to investment opportunities, often comparing the price and quality of available goods and services. One of the best-known aids in the effort to make purchases with foresight and knowledge is *Consumer Reports*, a 52-year-old publication that is a bible for serious, quality-conscious buyers. The monthly magazine is the primary project of an organization called Consumers Union (CU), whose statement of purpose is 'to provide consumers with information and advice on goods, services, health and personal finance; and to initiate and cooperate with individual and group efforts to maintain and enhance the quality of life for consumers.'

The first membership meeting of Consumers Union took place in 1937. Since then the organisation has earned worldwide respect while remaining true to a mission that has changed very little.

Consumer Reports enjoys a circulation of 3.8 million, placing it among the 20 most widely circulated magazines in the United States. In its 52 years, the magazine has carried test results on products ranging from breakfast cereals to lawn sprinklers, automobiles, binoculars, frozen fish fillets, dinette sets and space heaters to recent reports on videocassette recorders and mutual funds.

Consumers Union, however, despite its growth, remains a simple organization in the best sense. Its sole purpose is testing consumer goods. It accepts no advertising and limits the dollar amount of contributions it will accept from individuals to $1,000.

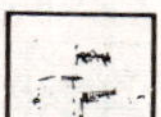
Selling products

Readers are almost uniform in their response to queries about why they buy *Consumer Reports*: They trust it and they know of no other readily accessible source for such thoroughly done and clearly presented research on questions of where they can get the best value for their money.

The Consumers Union laboratories are small and friendly, and the employees dress casually and go about their work at their own pace. It could be a college, except that today's test result could be tomorrow's headline; not just consumers, but American industry and the news media listen when CU speaks.

CU will test almost any kind of product except items such as alcohol, tobacco or firearms, which the board of directors decided not to report on lest it be construed that it was promoting their use.

Typical readers of *Consumer Reports* are well-educated and economically fairly welloff. Sixty per cent of the subscribers are men; 60 per cent have completed college; their average age is 41, and their median income is about 50 per cent above the American norm.

People who are not subscribers also use *Consumer Reports*, as it is available at most public libraries in the United States.

The esteem in which Americans hold Consumers Union reflects American regard for value, money, safety, endurance and, to some extent, prestige. The largest product testing organisation in the world (there are now 150 members in the International Organisation of Consumers Unions in 50 countries), Consumers Union is more than a useful institution; it has become a way of life.

Source: *Span*

c. *Answer the following questions based on the text:*

i. Why is *Consumer Reports* termed a bible for buyers?

ii. What is the objective of *Consumer Reports*?

iii. Why does Consumers Union not accept advertisements?

iv. What is meant by the statement, 'Today's test result could be tomorrow's headline'?

v. Are there things that Consumers Union will not test? What are they? Why will not these be tested?

vi. What are the ways in which people have access to *Consumer Reports*?

vii. What is meant by the statement, 'The Consumers Union is more than a useful institution; it has become a way of life'?

4. Discussion — 'Advertising style'

These are some common characteristics of advertisements.

conversational style
play on words

allusions to other contexts
superlatives
quoting facts and figures
paradox
....
....

You will find below five advertisements, which appeared in different publications. Choose one advertisement you like most and study its characteristics. Discuss in groups what you like most about its style, and then write down your conclusions. Be ready to report to the class when the teacher asks you.

PERSONAL CARE PRODUCTS PAR EXCELLENCE

HELENE CURTIS

The world won't stop because it's raining....
Aren't you glad there is
Duckback
Duckback
NYLON RAINWEAR
Made from tough, durable, 100% waterproof nylon material, in a range of smart designs and colours.
Lightweight and handy, Duckback Nylon Rainwear are supple enough to fold away neatly into any two-wheeler side compartment.
Bengal Waterproof Limited
41, Shakespeare Sarani, Calcutta-700 017
Showroom : 377, Dr. Dadabhai Nowroji Road, Bombay-400 001. Phone : 2049810, 2041487
Mileage/BW/89

Selling products

Follow-up

1. Oral practice

Student A: You are a customer interested in buying a refrigerator. A salesman has approached you offering the product of his company. Prepare a list of questions to ask him about the product.

Student B: You are a salesman interested in promoting the sales of the refrigerator of your company's make. You will be asked questions about your product by a prospective customer. Prepare yourself to answer them.

The questions and answers may be about the brand name of the refrigerator, its price, life span, guarantee period, features, advantages over other brands, etc. Start when you are both ready.

2. Writing skills development

Summarise into a brief passage the notes taken by you on page 204 listening to the talk on the export commitment of the Federation of Indian Chamber of Commerce and Industry.

3. Language development

Read the lists of advertisements and companies given below and match them.

Advertisements	*Companies*
Give with one hand Take with both	Hindustan Sugar Mills Ltd.
For 50 years, we have been making your life a lot sweeter	Limca

Slogans	Companies
Just 72 hours back this was an old, worn-out floor	Allwyn Trendy Quartz Coordinates
Thirst profession	Unit Trust of India
Discover 125 exciting ways to switch and match	Spartek
	Ceramics India Limited

4. Comprehension check

Look at the extracts from the text 'Direct Marketing' (page 207) produced below. Read the passage once again to see what these extracts refer to. Then answer the questions at the end of these extracts.

a. *The concept as yet remains half-baked.* (line 8) .... What concept?

b. *There must be some other way ... reaching one's specific target audience.* (line 4) .... Specific as different from what?

c. *It often causes delay in situations when time is crucial.* (line 22) .... What causes delay?

d. *It is on this mainspring ... the direct mail rests.* (line 34) .... What mainspring?